Lost in the Barrens

FARLEY MOWAT

Lost in the Barrens

ILLUSTRATED BY CHARLES GEER

McClelland and Stewart

Library of Congress Catalog Card No. 56-5628

Canadian trade and school paperback editions
published by arrangement with Atlantic-Little, Brown

School edition Notes and Activities copyright ©
1973, by McClelland and Stewart Limited

Trade paperback edition: 0-7710-6640-6

School paperback edition: 0-7710-6639-2

The Canadian Publishers
McClelland and Stewart Limited
25 Hollinger Road, Toronto

Manufactured in Canada by Webcom Limited

For ROBERT ALEXANDER MOWAT
  who will probably try to be one

For MURRAY BILOKI
  who would make a good one

For JACK MOWAT
  who is a real Indian already

Books by Farley Mowat

People of the Deer
The Regiment
The Dog Who Wouldn't Be
The Grey Seas Under
The Desperate People
The Serpent's Coil
Never Cry Wolf
Westviking
Canada North
This Rock Within the Sea
    (with John de Visser)
The Boat Who Wouldn't Float
Sibir
A Whale for the Killing
Wake of the Great Sealers (with David Blackwood)

FOR YOUNG READERS
Owls in the Family
Lost in the Barrens
The Black Joke
The Curse of the Viking Grave

EDITED BY FARLEY MOWAT
Coppermine Journey
The Top of the World trilogy
Ordeal by Ice
The Polar Passion
Tundra

Contents

CHAPTER 1

Jamie and Awasin

THE MONTH OF JUNE WAS GROW-
ing old. It had been a year since Jamie Macnair left Toronto, the city of his birth, to take up a new life in the
subarctic forests of northern Canada. Beside the shores of
Macnair Lake the tamaracks were greening now after the

3

winter's blackness. Out on the lake great loons cried shrilly. As Jamie squatted in front of the log cabin, helping his uncle bale up the winter's catch of furs, he tried to remember how he had felt on that day, a year past, when he climbed out of the train at the lonely frontier town called The Pas to meet his uncle.

Jamie's uncle, Angus Macnair, had been a trader in the arctic, the master of a sealing schooner in the Bering Sea, and finally a trapper who roamed over the broad forests of the north. To Jamie, his uncle was almost a legend, and when the telegram came from him it filled the boy with excitement.

ARRANGEMENTS MADE FOR YOU TO JOIN ME AT THE PAS STOP LETTER WITH DETAILS FOLLOWS.

ANGUS MACNAIR

That eagerly awaited letter had brought with it some unhappiness for Jamie. It had reminded him sharply of the tragedy of his parents' deaths in a car accident seven years ago. And it had made clear something he had never really faced before — that apart from his uncle, whom he had never seen, he was truly alone. During the past seven years he had taken the security of the boarding school for granted. But, reading Angus Macnair's letter, he realized that it was no real home, and had never been one.

Jamie was nine when his parents died, and Angus Macnair had become his guardian, for he was the boy's only close relative. It was Angus who had picked the boarding school in Toronto, and it was a good one too, for Angus

4

wanted only the best for his nephew. For seven years Angus had run his trap line with furious energy in order to meet the cost of the school. But in the past two years the fur market had dropped almost out of sight, and the money was nearly at an end.

Angus had explained it in his letter.

"And so you see, Jamie," he wrote. "I can no longer keep you at the school. You could maybe stay on in Toronto and get a job, but you're too young for that, and anyhow I hoped you'd rather come with me. It's long past time we got to know each other. So I took the chance you'd want it this way. Your ticket is in the envelope along with enough money for the trip. And I'll be waiting, lad, and hoping that you'll come."

Angus need have had no doubts. For years past Jamie had loved to read about the north and for years Angus Macnair had been his idol.

In the last week of June, Jamie found himself bundled aboard the Trans-Canada train with the farewells of his school friends still ringing in his ears. For two days the train rolled westward, then it turned abruptly north through the province of Manitoba. The dark jack-pine forests began to swallow up the prairie farmlands and the train rolled on, more slowly now, over the rough roadbed leading to the frontier country.

Five hundred miles and two days north from Winnipeg, the train drew up by a rough wooden platform. Jamie climbed uncertainly down to stand staring at the rough shanties and the nearby forests that threatened to sweep in and engulf the little settlement of The Pas.

A huge, red-bearded man in a buckskin jacket strode forward and caught the boy hard about the shoulders in a bear hug.

"Do ye not know me, Jamie?" he cried. And then, grinning at Jamie's stammering reply, he tightened his hold on the boy's shoulder and swung him round.

"You've come to meet the north, my lad," he said, "and I'm thinking you'll be in love with it before the month is out."

Angus Macnair had been a good prophet, for during the six-week canoe trip north to Macnair Lake, Jamie had become fascinated by the wild face of this new world. Now, a year later, he was really a part of that world. The year in the forests had swelled his shoulders with new muscles so that he looked taller than his five-foot-eight. Summer suns and winter winds had tanned his face. His blue eyes were sharp and alert under his tousled mat of fair hair.

And the little cabin by the shores of the lake had become his home — his first real home since his parents died.

Built within a stone's throw of the sandy shore, the cabin was nevertheless almost surrounded by the sheltering forests. No winter gales could reach it, and the log walls, well chinked with moss and clay, were proof against the sharpest frosts. Crouched comfortably among the trees, it looked out through two small windows over a lake that was a glittering expanse of blue in summer and a vast white plain in winter.

6

Inside, it was divided into two rooms. The largest was the living room. It had two bunks built against the side walls. A potbellied Quebec heater stood in the center of the floor, glowing cherry-red in the winter days. Beside the stove a long, roughhewn table stretched almost across the room and at either end of it stood a big, homemade easy chair upholstered with black-bear hide. Shelves along the rough log walls held guns, a number of wood carvings done by the Indians, and the well-worn rows of Angus's books. On the split-log floors half a dozen Indian-tanned deer hides made soft rugs.

The tiny kitchen in the rear was cut off from the main cabin by a log partition, and behind the partition Angus cooked the solid and simple meals of the northland.

Although the cabin was four hundred miles from civilization, and two hundred miles from the nearest white man, Jamie had not found it lonely. Not twenty miles away was the settlement of a band of Woodland Cree Indians. These fine and sturdy people had long been Angus Macnair's best friends and they soon became Jamie's friends as well. Alphonse Meewasin, headman of the Crees, had been Angus's stout companion on a hundred journeys and it was only natural that Alphonse's son, Awasin, should become almost a brother to young Jamie.

In appearance Awasin was Jamie's opposite. He was lean as a whip, with long black hair that hung almost to his shoulders. His eyes too were black, and they smiled as often as his mouth — and that was very often. For three seasons Awasin had attended the Indian school in far-off

Pelican Narrows, so that he could read and speak English almost as well as any city boy. But most of his life had been lived in the heart of the forests and the wilderness was as much a part of him as his own skin.

Jamie and Awasin had taken to each other at once, and Awasin had appointed himself Jamie's teacher. Quickly Jamie became competent with a paddle and at driving a string of dogs. He learned to shoot well and he learned enough about trapping to earn the money for a .22 rifle of his own. Most important, under the instruction of Awasin and of Angus Macnair, Jamie learned to feel something of the forceful love of life that belongs particularly to those who dwell in the high arctic forests.

It had been a year filled to the brim with new adventures, and as Jamie wound a rawhide strap around a pile of muskrat pelts his imagination was reliving those events. With a start he looked up to see a slim cedar canoe rounding a nearby point.

Awasin was in the bow, waving his paddle in greeting. And in the stern Alphonse stolidly chewed his old pipe as he thrust his paddle into the icy waters of the lake.

CHAPTER 2

The Camp of the Crees

THE MEEWASINS, FATHER AND SON, were frequent visitors to the Macnair cabin, but this morning they had come for a special reason. Alphonse had long suspected that the nearest fur trader, two hundred miles south, was cheating the Crees. He had spoken of his suspicions to Angus, and at last Angus had suggested that Alphonse should go with him on the long trip south to The Pas, where there was an honest market. After conference with the hunters of his band, Alphonse had decided to take his friend's advice.

Alphonse's decision meant that Angus's original plans for the journey south now had to be altered. He had intended to take Jamie with him, but even his big freight canoe would not carry all the Cree furs, the two men, and Jamie. So it was arranged that Jamie would remain with Alphonse's family at the Cree camp on nearby Thanout Lake until the two men returned, six or eight weeks later.

"I hope you'll not mind missing the trip, Jamie," Angus said.

Jamie shook his head emphatically. "Awasin and I will have a better time right here."

Angus was well pleased at Jamie's willingness to stay in the forests rather than visit civilization again.

"Good lad!" he said. "I'll not forget ye when I do the shopping in The Pas. There'll be a brand-new hunting rifle for ye in my pack when I get home and in the meantime you can use my thirty-thirty, for a woodsman should have a real rifle of his own."

Jamie straightened his shoulders with pride, for this loan of a heavy-caliber rifle meant that Angus considered him to be almost a man.

"You'll do well enough when I'm gone," Angus continued, "but remember one thing. Awasin knows more about the north than you'll ever know. He'll be the boss, and if ye forget it, I'll remind you with the flat of my paddle when I get back again!"

10

Awasin took immediate advantage of Angus's command. "That's right!" he said. "I'm boss. So you go down to the canoe and clean those fish we brought for supper!"

"Hey!" Jamie cried indignantly. "That's not what my uncle meant! Last one to the canoe cleans the fish himself!"

The boys raced down the slope, collided near the canoe and fell together in a rough-and-tumble wrestling match.

Alphonse watched with a smile. "When the dog pup and the fox cub play together, the gods are pleased," he said. "Those two will come to no harm. But in any case, my brother Solomon will watch them, and my wife will see to it that they lack for nothing."

Three days later the big canoe pulled away from the shores of Thanout Lake, loaded to the gunwales with bales of fur. Awasin and Jamie watched it out of sight, in company with the men and women of the Cree camp. Then they turned up the shady slope where the dozen log cabins of the Crees nestled against the dark green forests.

Jamie had looked forward to a summer of fishing, hunting and exploring with Awasin, but soon he found that plans were being made for him by other people. Marie Meewasin, Alphonse's fat and jovial wife, kept the two boys busy from dawn till dusk. Fish nets had to be tended, wood gathered, dogs fed. A dozen other tasks filled the daylight hours.

In exchange for all this, Marie fed the boys hot bannocks made from flour, baking powder, water and sugar;

11

roast lake trout and whitefish; fried deermeat or spruce grouse; and gallons of the hot, sweet tea the Indians love so well.

It was a good life, but such a busy one that Jamie's dreams of an exploring expedition seemed doomed. Always there was work to be done. Three weeks passed and it was well into July. Then one evening Awasin's Uncle Solomon appeared unexpectedly in the cabin door.

Solomon spoke abruptly. "There are visitors upon the lake," he said. "Three canoes of the Deer Eaters come from the north. They will land in an hour's time and you, Awasin, must greet them on the shore, for you are the Chief's son."

He vanished and Jamie asked, "*Who* are the Deer Eaters, Awasin?"

Awasin was frowning. "They are the Idthen Eldeli, a band of Chipeweyans who live about a hundred miles north of us. In the old days we used to fight them. But Alphonse made friends with them a long time back, and now they sometimes pay us a visit. Usually when something's wrong."

Awasin bolted down the rest of his supper and started for the door. "You stay here!" he said over his shoulder to Jamie, and his words were an order.

Jamie muttered rebelliously, but did as he had been told. He stood in the doorway and watched three birch-bark canoes paddle leisurely out of the evening mist toward the shore. Two men were in each canoe, small men dressed entirely in deerskin clothing instead of in blue

12

jeans and bright cotton shirts like the Crees who waited on the beach.

When they were a few feet from land the visitors let their canoes drift. One of them called out a greeting in a deep, guttural voice. Instantly Awasin answered in the same strange language. The canoes landed and the six Idthen Eldeli hunters climbed out and stood facing the group of waiting Crees.

A number of Cree women now hurried down to the shore carrying fish, flour and tea. The Chipeweyans started a fire and in a short time they were eating ravenously while their leader stood apart with Awasin and Solomon. The strange chief, Denikazi, was a powerful, squat man of middle age with very dark skin that had been pitted by smallpox.

At last he and Awasin, with Solomon following, came up the slope and entered the cabin. Denikazi's jet-black eyes flickered over Jamie briefly, then ignored him. Jamie sat quietly in a corner while Marie made tea and the men talked in the Chipeweyan tongue.

An hour later, when Denikazi had gone back to his own men, Awasin satisfied Jamie's curiosity about the visit.

Denikazi was chief of the Kasmere Lake band of Chipeweyans who lived on the edge of the Barrenland plains. They were called Deer Eaters because their whole lives were dependent on the caribou — a kind of reindeer found in the high arctic in immense herds.

The caribou spend the summers out on the plains, but in the fall they migrate by the tens of thousands into the

13

forests, where they spend the winter. The Chipeweyans eat almost nothing but deermeat and bannocks. The only trapping they do is to kill enough white foxes to trade for ammunition and a little flour and tea.

The preceding winter had been a bad one for foxes, and as a result, Denikazi's band had no pelts to trade for ammunition. The fur trader refused to give them credit, so that spring the Deer Eaters had been unable to kill enough caribou to last through the summer. Now famine was upon them and already the dogs were starving to death. The people would soon starve too, and so Denikazi had come to his ancient enemies, the Crees, for help.

"They need food to last a month, and shells as well," Awasin continued. "Denikazi plans to take a hunting party right out into the Barrenlands to find the deer on the summer range and bring home enough dried meat to last till fall. He must be really desperate to risk going into the plains. That's Eskimo country. Once, a long time ago, the Chips used to hunt out there regularly, but they used to fight the Eskimos whenever they met. In those days the Chips had rifles and the Eskimos didn't. Then the Eskimos got rifles and fought back. The Idthen Eldeli haven't dared go far out in the plains since."

"Are you going to help them?" Jamie wanted to know.

Awasin's mouth set stubbornly. "Yes," he replied. "My Uncle Solomon doesn't think we should. He says it's probably just a trick to get things from us. But my father has never turned a hungry man away."

Marie came to Awasin's side. She put her hand on his

shoulder and spoke softly to him. "You are your mother's son as well," she said, "and no one of our race has ever refused food to those who starve!"

Awasin smiled up at her. "I'm sure it's no trick, Mother," he said, "but if it is — I know a way to find out. I could go back with the Chips to Kasmere Lake and *see* how bad things are. I'd carry the ammunition in my own canoe, and if Denikazi really needs it, then I can hand it over."

Jamie jumped to his feet. "You mean *we'll* go!" he shouted. "You don't leave *me* behind!"

Marie laughed. "I think my son thought of this plan just to get out of work," she said. "But it is a good plan for it will settle Solomon's doubts. Also it will get you two out from under my feet for a few days. Denikazi will let no harm come to a son of Alphonse Meewasin."

"Then we *can* go?" Awasin cried.

His mother nodded her head.

Fairly stuttering with excitement, the two boys raced out of the cabin to spread the news. Marie watched them from the doorway, with a broad smile.

CHAPTER 3

To the Camps of the Deer Eaters

THE SUN WAS STILL BELOW THE
horizon when Awasin shook his friend awake. Marie had
tea and a big pan of fried fish all ready on the table.
The boys wolfed down the food, picked up their packsacks, and hurried out into the gray light to where the
canoes lay drawn up on the sandy shore.

The Chipeweyans were busy loading their own canoes with sacks of dried deermeat, flour and fish — all gifts from the Cree band. A few yards to one side the Crees were grouped about a slender seventeen-foot canvas-covered cedar canoe which the boys were to use. Marie, Awasin, and his Uncle Solomon had been up half the night preparing and loading it.

Carefully stowed in the canoe's bottom were two bed-rolls of heavy woolen blankets, a short length of gill net for fishing in deep water, a hand line and spare hooks, a small ax, a canvas tarpaulin to cover the load or to be used as a tent, and a fifty-foot length of half-inch rope for use in "tracking" the canoe up rapids.

Marie had arranged the food with a generous hand, for the boys were to travel into a starvation area and they would need to carry all their supplies with them. In the wooden "grub box" Marie had packed salt, sugar, baking powder, lard, flour, tea and a can of honey, in addition to a big sack of dry meat.

In their packsacks they had spare socks, three extra pairs of moose-hide moccasins apiece, sweaters, spare shirts, six boxes of .30-30 shells each and a sewing kit. The twenty extra boxes of ammunition for Denikazi were packed in the bow.

For cooking equipment the boys carried an iron frying pan and an old sirup can, blackened by many fires, which could be used either as a tea can or "tea-billy," as a stew-pot, or as a water pail. Matches were stored in three little glass bottles.

Even in midsummer, mornings in the northern forests can be cold, and so the boys were dressed in heavy canvas trousers, thick woolen shirts, and windbreakers of light canvas. On their feet they wore thick socks, rolled up over their trouser cuffs, and moose-hide moccasins slipped into ordinary black rubbers such as city dwellers wear over their shoes on rainy days.

The first yellow light of dawn was breaking as the boys and Denikazi's men climbed silently into their canoes and the Crees pushed them away from shore. Despite the quiet, Jamie felt a thrill of anticipation as he took his place in the bow of the cedar canoe.

Marie called out some last-minute advice. Some of the Crees made joking remarks about the boys' canoemanship. Then the Chipeweyans were leaning forward, their powerful arms driving their paddles deep into the still waters. Hurriedly Jamie and Awasin picked up the rhythm, and in a few moments the four canoes were slipping into the misty distances that stretched toward the north.

The Chipeweyans, skilled canoe men, and driven by the urgency of their mission, forged far ahead of the two boys. Wasting no breath on words, Jamie and Awasin paddled with all their strength, and despite the chill of the mist, sweat soon stood on their foreheads.

Jamie's lips set stubbornly. "We've got to catch them," he said grimly. "Let's get going!"

Each boy paddled three strokes on one side of the canoe, then, flipping his paddle into the air, caught it and came down on the other side without missing a stroke.

18

The frequent change of side meant that their muscles had no chance to grow strained in one position, and the steady rhythm of the motion made the work seem easier.

At first the canoes were gliding under the early morning shadow cast by the high banks of the lake. Toward noon they came abreast of a clearing that held the crumbled walls of an abandoned cabin. The Chipeweyan canoes swung out into the lake, giving the desolate place a wide berth.

The boys both knew the story of the deserted cabin. It had been built by a red-headed young Englishman as an outpost trading station. But for almost twenty years it had stood abandoned. No one knew for certain what happened to the young trader, but the Crees had a story that he had set out one winter to trade for white fox pelts with the Eskimos, and had never returned. The only memory of him was in this pile of rotted logs still called Red-Head Post.

"The Chipeweyans act as if they're nervous of Red-Head Post," Jamie commented as they paddled by.

Awasin was slow to answer. "Perhaps they know something about the trader's disappearance that nobody else knows," he replied. "They're a queer people."

Dusk was falling before the canoes reached the north end of the lake. This was where the boys would leave behind the lands they knew and enter the unknown wilderness.

The canoes nosed into a tiny sand beach where the Idthen Eldeli always began the long portage around the Kasmere Falls. It was too late that night to make the "carry," so the campfires were lighted on the beach. The boys sat at Denikazi's fire eating roast whitefish. When the meal was finished the Indian leader walked away without a word and rolled himself in his blankets.

The boys went back to their canoe, turned it over on the sand, and crawled underneath. They pulled the blankets up about their faces to keep the mosquitoes away. The distant quaver of a wolf drifted through the darkness but the boys did not hear, for they were already asleep.

Long before dawn they were awake again. Denikazi was in such a driving hurry to reach his own camps that he begrudged every moment wasted on the way. There was no breakfast — only a handful of dry meat to chew as the men and boys began the long portage.

Jamie volunteered to carry the canoe, but before he had gone a mile he repented his eagerness. The route was an obstacle course, strewn with fire-felled logs and swampy muskeg holes. With the canoe balanced on his back, he leaped from log to log and from hummock to hummock. To make things worse a plague of black flies attacked them.

Awasin carried the two packsacks and all the rest of the gear. He was loaded like a mule.

It took two hours to complete the carry. When at last they reached the banks of the Kasmere River they were exhausted. But already the Chipeweyan canoes were in the current. Denikazi gave them no time to rest. His harsh, pock-scarred face betrayed no sympathy as he gave the order to take to the river.

Downstream into the north the canoes fled like sparrows chased by hawks. The pine and spruce forests on either bank slid past so rapidly they seemed blurred as the boys kept their eyes glued to the river and to the erratic motions of the Chipeweyan canoe immediately ahead.

The first rapid leaped at them, a roaring canyon of foam and tortured water. In the bow, Jamie worked furiously to keep the head of the canoe away from the black rocks that raced toward him. Awasin, in the stern, paddled with all his strength to keep steerageway so that they could slide from side to side of the narrow, rock-filled channels.

One rapid followed another until noon, when the current began to die away and the river broadened into a bay. Ahead, stretching twin arms into the north, lay Kasmere Lake.

After a short halt to eat, they were off across the great lake. The hours went by monotonously. By the time the sun dropped behind the sparsely wooded hills to the west, the Chipeweyan canoes had drawn miles ahead. The boys were alone in the darkening wilderness.

Then Awasin's quick eye picked out a number of tiny whitish blobs against the black shadows of the forests ahead. "There's Denikazi's camp!" he cried. "I see the tents!"

As they approached the shore, the crimson sparkle of

campfires grew and spread. A chorus of dog howls echoed across the water and the steady beat of an Indian drum rolled out over the still lake.

The boys stopped paddling and let the canoe drift to shore. Ahead of them was a long sand bar upon which stood a dozen squat, cone-shaped tents. Cooking fires burned, sending strange shadows dancing on the walls of the tepees and illuminating the figures of twenty or thirty people standing motionless at the water's edge.

It was a wild and barbaric sight. In this tent-camp of the Idthen Eldeli men lived a life that had been almost unchanged for a thousand years. Though they had rifles now instead of bows and arrows, they were untouched by most of the ways of the white man's world. They lived in the old way, and worshiped the ancient gods.

As the canoe drifted uncertainly, the boys were hailed by the strong voice of Denikazi. In Chipeweyan he called, "Who comes?"

Awasin replied in the same tongue. "Sons of Enna, the Crees, come from afar!"

At the sound of Awasin's ritual reply a great shout rose. It echoed out over the still water and pierced the gathering darkness.

"Friends come upon us! Lay down the bows!"

It was the ancient phrase with which the Idthen Eldeli had greeted their friends for uncounted generations.

A little frightened by the strangeness of it all, Jamie stepped cautiously out of the canoe. Denikazi led the boys to his own tent, where a fire burned high and bright. Two

22

women appeared carrying wooden trays filled with boiled fish and dry deermeat, part of the gift from the Crees. Knowing how hungry the Chipeweyan camp was supposed to be, Jamie was about to refuse the food, but Awasin whispered quickly:

"Take it, Jamie. They are offering the best they have, to show that we are welcome. If you refuse they will be angry."

The boys helped themselves sparingly while the Chipeweyan chief watched silently. Not until they had finished their meal did Denikazi speak. Then he stood up beside the fire and faced them.

"When my father's fathers went to the land of the Enna," he began, "they received only the sharp wounds of arrows. That was a long time since. Now I have gone to the Enna and I have received food and friendship both. I will not forget this thing. Therefore remember: in this place and in this land you are the brothers of my people — and the sons of Denikazi!"

Abruptly the chief turned from them and strode toward a distant fire where a squatting circle of men awaited him. The boys slowly followed at a discreet distance.

Cautiously they walked along the row of tents toward the conference fire. The gaunt faces and thin bodies of the few people at the tents sharply confirmed Denikazi's story of starvation. The tents themselves were made entirely of roughly scraped deer hides stretched over a framework of spruce poles. One or two had their door flaps flung back and Jamie could see that they were al-

23

most empty. A few deer-hide robes, a rusty rifle, a pile of old skin clothing and perhaps a battered wooden box made up the furnishings. He had never seen such poverty before, and he was shocked by it.

He was not surprised when Awasin said, "There is no doubt, Jamie, they are in trouble. We will hand the ammunition over in the morning."

Now the boys were close to the great fire where Denikazi and the Idthen Eldeli men were gathered. Here were the hunters of the camp — small, wiry men, with hungry faces. One or two turned suspicious, watchful eyes on the boys, then ignored them.

Denikazi spoke and was answered by one of his men. It was all meaningless to Jamie until Awasin suddenly stiffened and his hand clutched Jamie's arm so hard it hurt.

"What's the matter?" Jamie whispered.

"They are planning the deer hunt out in the Barrens," Awasin replied in a tense voice, "and they seem to think we are going with them!"

It took a moment for the startling idea to register on Jamie's mind; then he reacted. A wave of excitement swept over him. Here was the possibility of real adventure. Visions of the vast and unknown plains of the arctic with their tremendous herds of caribou flashed before his eyes.

"Well?" he said breathlessly. "Why not?"

Awasin did not reply. In the flush of his enthusiasm Jamie rushed on. "We can get them to send a message back saying we're going. Nobody will worry about us, and we'll be back in a couple of weeks." He paused but still Awasin did not reply. "What about it?" Jamie urged. "We'll never get another chance like this!"

Awasin was a cautious lad. Jamie could throw himself into wild adventures — but if anything went wrong, it would be Awasin who was responsible. Awasin knew that neither his father nor Angus Macnair would approve. And yet his desire to see the Barrenlands was as great as Jamie's.

Exasperated by his friend's silence, Jamie said the first thing that came into his mind.

"You aren't afraid, are you?" he whispered sharply.

Awasin spun about, and even in the dim light of the fire Jamie saw the harsh gleam in his friend's dark eyes.

"We'll go!" Awasin almost hissed. "And we'll find out who's frightened."

But Awasin's anger did not last. It may be that he was glad the decision had been forced upon him.

In the morning Awasin talked with Denikazi for some time and then told Jamie all he could gather about the expedition. It was clear that the main reason the Chipeweyans wanted the two boys along was because of their good .30-30 rifles. The Chipeweyan guns were old, rusted and almost useless except at close range. The boys' guns might mean the difference between failure and success, and Denikazi could not afford to let the hunt fail. But he made it clear that the boys must agree to obey his word in everything. He put it this way to Awasin: "The old wolf leads and the young wolves follow!" And Awasin knew that an old wolf whose authority is challenged can be an ugly customer.

Rather grudgingly Denikazi arranged for a messenger to travel down to Thanout Lake carrying a letter from Awasin to his mother. The letter was vague because the boys could not predict how the hunt would develop. Denikazi would only say that they might be gone for "half the life of the new moon," or roughly two weeks.

Actually Denikazi himself could not know how long he would be gone. His plan was to go north at top speed to a place which lay just outside the forests. Here he hoped to meet the deer moving southward. But if the deer had not yet arrived, Denikazi would have to push further north into the open plains. The caribou make a midsummer migration from the far north down almost to timber line each year; then they go north again for a month or so until the snow finally drives them south to spend the winter inside the forests. Denikazi had to intercept this midsummer migration if his people were to have enough food to last till winter. To him, the time he would be gone was not important. He would be gone until he had loaded his canoes with meat.

Because they wanted to, the boys convinced themselves that the hunt would last two weeks at the most.

CHAPTER 4

North to the Barrenlands

THERE WAS VERY LITTLE CERE-
mony about the departure of Denikazi and his hunters for
the mysterious lands to the north. Their flotilla consisted
of four canoes, each about sixteen feet long, made of
slabs of birch bark sewed with sinew thread and water-
proofed with spruce gum. Two hunters manned each

27

canoe and they carried only a few deerskin robes and their hunting equipment. They would have to live off the land. The boys, of course, traveled in their own canoe and with their own equipment.

They left the camp at dawn and paddled only a few miles on Kasmere Lake before entering a little stream that came swirling down out of the northwest. Here there was a halt and Denikazi spoke to the two boys.

"Ahead of us lie many portages up the White-Partridge River," he began. "Beyond the river lies Kazba-tua, White-Partridge Lake, and there the forests die. From this time on you are but two of my men and you will do as I choose."

The party's progress up White-Partridge River consisted of much walking, and very little paddling. The portages were over shattered rock or across soggy muskegs and even the Chipeweyan men, with their light loads, found it hard. For the boys it was a nightmare endurance test. By dusk they were staggering with fatigue and had fallen several miles behind the Chipeweyans. They camped alone by the shores of a little lake.

After eating they sat beside a tiny fire — for already the forests were dwindling and dry wood was hard to find. The loneliness and immensity of the new wilderness seemed to close down upon them. As cheerfully as they could they unrolled their bedrolls under the upturned canoe, and when they slept it was a sleep of pure exhaustion.

In the morning when they awoke, stiff and chilled, they

discovered that their fire was burning brightly and Denikazi was squatting beside it. On a forked stick slanting over the coals a fat whitefish sizzled — one of a number of fish the Chipeweyans had caught that night in a net.

As the boys scrambled to their feet, shamefaced at having overslept, Denikazi spoke. "We wait at the next portage," he said, and walked away.

Jamie shook his head in surprise. "I don't understand," he said wonderingly. "He should have been mad at us for holding up the trip — and instead he brings us a fresh fish for breakfast."

"Denikazi is all right," Awasin replied as he pulled the hot fish off the stick and divided it. "He is worried and that's why he seems so hard."

"Then let's not be a drag on him," Jamie said. "Let's show him we know how to travel too!"

Less than half an hour later they arrived at the portage and the Chipeweyan chief showed clearly he was pleased at the speed they had made.

The hard work of the previous day began once more. Small, shallow lakes succeeded each other, and in between were unmarked portages. But now the forests had almost disappeared and the land was opening up as if a curtain were being raised. The hilltops were bare, and the isolated patches of forest in the valleys were composed only of stunted little spruces. The ground was rocky, with nothing but lichens and mosses to cover its harsh face.

A day passed and then another. Then a vast hill loomed high on the horizon like a huge, bald dome. Denikazi

29

recognized it with a grunt of pleasure. "Kazba-seth!" he cried. White-Partridge Mountain. "Beyond lies Kazba-tua and there we will find deep waters for our paddles."

When the canoes took to the water the next morning, the summer was half over. The caribou herds should already be headed south out of the vast plains. Hunters and hunted were moving steadily toward each other, but not even Denikazi could tell where, or when, they would meet.

Near the head of Kazba-tua was the Place of the New Fawns, where — in times past — the Chipeweyan hunters had met the southbound herds and speared untold numbers of caribou as the beasts swam the current. This place was Denikazi's immediate objective and now he led the way toward it at a swift pace.

On the evening of the second day the canoes ran up a long, narrow bay that funneled into a canyon with sheer walls. The throaty roar of swift water told the hunters that here was the beginning of a mighty river. Only Denikazi knew its name. Kazon-dee-zee, the Long River, he called it. At the mouth of Kazon-dee-zee lay the Place of the New Fawns. The Indians approached it with a tense expectation, scanning the rolling plains for signs of caribou. The plains were somber, lifeless, and empty of the deer. The Indians' disappointment must have been terrible, but they showed no trace of their true feelings.

At three o'clock the next morning Denikazi gave the

order to move on. Dawn had already broken, since this far north there was very little darkness.

The boys hurried to get ready, for they had no desire to be left behind. They were shocked when they saw what lay ahead of them. The Kazon River looked like a slalom course down a mountainside. It roared over a jumbled mass of glacial boulders that tore the water into high-flung sheets of foam.

By the time the boys' canoe had reached the mouth of the river, the other canoes had already reached the brink of this maelstrom. Denikazi led the way down an oily funnel of water at the head of the first rapid. His canoe hung poised for an instant, then, as if plucked up and flung by a giant hand, the frail bark vessel shot forward and disappeared into a thundering mass of spray. It reappeared a moment later racing downstream at breakneck speed, and twisting and turning like a frightened fish. Then, while the boys stared in horror, the canoe emerged unharmed in a quiet eddy at the foot of the rapids.

The others followed without hesitation. Jamie felt a hard, tight knot forming in his stomach.

"Think we can make it?" he asked feebly.

Awasin looked grim. "We'd better!" he replied shortly.

They eased their canoe into the channel. Suddenly the rocky banks began to shoot past like twin express trains on either side. The canoe appeared motionless while the world went crazy. A frothing caldron of foam leaped up in front of Jamie and he flailed his paddle desperately in order to swing the nose of the canoe away. Instantly a row of black rocks raced at him, and with frantic heaves he thrust the canoe back to the right again. He was startled when the canoe suddenly came to a level keel, and the shore stopped flashing past.

It was over. The Chipeweyans waited nearby.

The first rapid on a new river always seems the worst. Once it has been conquered, the rest are easier. By mid-afternoon the boys had run three formidable rapids and a dozen smaller ones. They were cocky and full of high spirits when they camped that night. In the morning they would again be on open water — on Idthen-tua, at whose northern end they were certain they would meet the deer at last.

CHAPTER 5

Of Eskimos and Indians

WHEN MORNING CAME IT BROUGHT with it heavy cloud and flying rain-scud. Despite the fact that it was still summer, there was a chill in the air.

The boys hastened to a tiny willow fire where the seven hunters were huddled together trying to get dry. Denikazi was not there. Suddenly Awasin pointed, and nudged Jamie.

On a hillock a hundred yards from camp the chief stood against the gray sky like a squat, powerful monument of

33

rock. His hands were uplifted and his voice cried out over the dark landscape. Denikazi was calling on his gods — ancient gods — for help in finding the deer. Denikazi was worried. Already he had been gone for more than a week and he had found no sign of the deer herds.

It was not that the country ahead was unfamiliar. Denikazi knew the plains well enough to find his way about. There was another thing which worried him — the Eskimos.

But he was a brave man, and he had to go on if his people were to be saved from death. All that morning he prayed to his gods and meditated. At noon his decision was made.

He would go on. He would drive north until he found the deer. He would ignore the danger of the Eskimos.

Denikazi called the two boys before him and explained his plan. He told them in detail of the Eskimo danger. He made it clear that from this moment on he and his men would not have a moment to spare for the boys. He threatened that if they got left behind, they would have to look after themselves.

But if he thought the boys would be frightened and choose to wait at the south end of Idthen-tua, he was mistaken.

"Tell him we're not afraid of any Eskimos," Jamie said.

Awasin translated Jamie's words while Denikazi listened stolidly. He looked at Jamie and there was a hint of humor in his black eyes.

"A fool you may well be," he said slowly, "but a brave

34

fool. You may come to the head of Idthen-tua, but no farther. Follow the east shore of the lake. You will not have
me to guide you for I wait for no one now."

When the boys crawled out from their sleeping robes
the next morning they found the camp deserted. Denikazi's canoes had already vanished in the broad sweep of
water to the north.

They hurried their morning meal and took to the water,
anxious to close the gap between themselves and the only
other friendly human beings in the waste of rock and
moss.

Hugging the rocky eastern shore, the canoe crawled
northward. The boys stared intently at the land about for
signs of life, but nothing moved except the birds. Muskeg
succeeded muskeg, and Jamie noticed that these expanses
of sodden moss appeared to have been cut up into millions
of tiny squares and rectangles by dark streaks. It was a
mystery, until noon when the boys landed to make tea.
Then the mystery explained itself. The muskegs were
crisscrossed by countless paths made by the hoofs of the
deer. Jamie's imagination was stunned as he tried to visual-
ize the size of the herds that must have passed this way
each year for centuries. Both he and Awasin felt now that
come what might they *must* see with their own eyes those
almost legendary hordes of caribou. They hurried back
to the canoe and continued north with new energy and
enthusiasm. At this very moment the herds might be
sweeping down upon the north end of the lake.

Toward evening the lake began to narrow rapidly until

it was only a few miles across and the land to the west was taking shape. Knowing that they must be near their goal, the boys paddled wearily on until nearly midnight, when a flicker of orange flame against the shadows ahead told them they had reached Denikazi's camp.

Jamie was so tired he stumbled out of the canoe. With Awasin he made his way toward the fire.

The Chipeweyans were grouped morosely about a tiny flame. Denikazi, sitting to one side, had his head in his hands. No one spoke to the two boys.

They did not need to ask if the deer had come. The atmosphere of gloom and depression in the camp spoke louder than words. The boys said nothing, but returned to their canoe and curled up under it to sleep the dreamless sleep of complete exhaustion.

This camp had been pitched at a spot known to the ancient Chipeweyan hunters as the Killing Place. But during the two days which followed there were no deer at the river, and none on the plains about. The skies clouded over and a steady rain beat down. Food was running low. The Indians set a net at the mouth of the Kazon, but the total catch for three days was a single sucker.

Denikazi remained silent. Once he walked to the crest of a nearby hill, and through a gap in the low clouds Jamie saw him standing there with his arms upraised to the dark sky. But the deer did not come.

On the third day the skies cleared. Denikazi called the men and the boys about him.

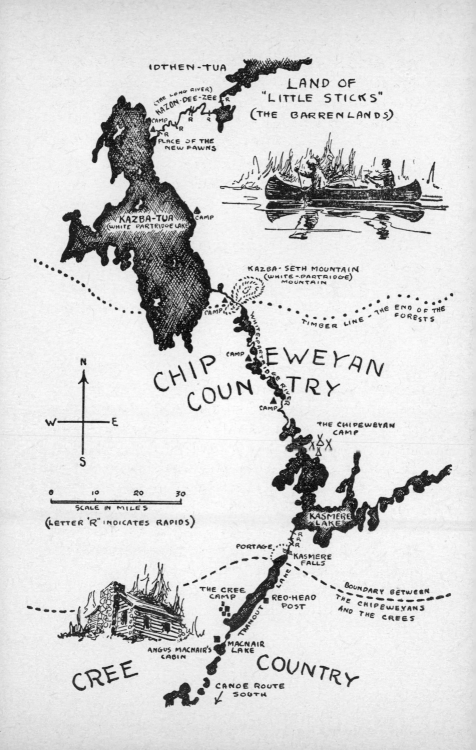

IDTHEN-TUA

LAND OF
"LITTLE STICKS"
(THE BARRENLANDS)

(THE LONG RIVER)
KAZON-DEE-ZEE R R
R R
CAMP
R
PLACE OF THE
NEW FAWNS

KAZBA-TUA
(WHITE PARTRIDGE LAKE) CAMP

KAZBA-SETH MOUNTAIN
(WHITE-PARTRIDGE)
MOUNTAIN

CAMP

TIMBER LINE - THE END OF THE
FORESTS

CAMP

WHITEPARTRIDGE RIVER

CHIPEWEYAN
COUNTRY

N
W E
S

CAMP

THE CHIPEWEYAN
CAMP

0 10 20 30
SCALE IN MILES

(LETTER 'R' INDICATES RAPIDS)

KASMERE
LAKE

PORTAGE
R
R
R
KASMERE
FALLS

BOUNDARY BETWEEN
THE CHIPEWEYANS
AND THE CREES

THE CREE
CAMP
RED-HEAD
POST

THANOUT LAKE

ANGUS MACNAIR'S
CABIN
MACNAIR
LAKE

CREE COUNTRY

CANOE ROUTE
SOUTH

"There have been great changes in the way of things since I was a youth," he began slowly, "and it seems that the deer too have changed their ways. Perhaps they will come to the Killing Place in time — but we cannot wait for them. By Kasmere Lake my people starve. And to the north, somewhere there is meat. Therefore I shall go north and find that meat. It is better for hunters to die on the trail than to wait like children in the camps."

Then Denikazi told them of his plan. He and three of his men would go back down Idthen-tua to the western arm, then up it to its end. Old tribal legends told of a chain of lakes that led northward from there to the high blue hills of To-bon-tua — the lake that never thaws. The River of the Frozen Lake began under those hills — one of which could be clearly seen from the present camp.

This hill loomed up almost due north of the Killing Place, perhaps thirty or forty miles away. Beyond it to the west the River of the Frozen Lake lay in a great valley down which — so it was said — all the deer of the entire northern plains came pouring in the fall.

Denikazi was certain that if he could reach the valley he would be able to fill his canoes with meat.

Jamie listened fascinated as Awasin explained Denikazi's plan. Then he asked a question.

"Wouldn't it be quicker and easier to reach the valley simply by going north up the Kazon, then portaging west to the mountain we can see from here?" he asked.

"Beyond this camp the Kazon belongs to the Eskimos," Denikazi replied. "We stand on the very edge of their lands and to go farther into it would mean an end to all our hunting."

Denikazi looked at Jamie and Awasin. "As for you," he said, "you will stay here. Telie-kwazie and Etzanni will remain with you, and for six days you will wait at the Killing Place for the deer. If they do not come within that time, you will travel south to the mouth of the western arm of Idthen-tua and wait for me there. If, in fifteen days, my canoe does not come to you, then you will go home — alone. And at Kasmere Lake you will tell my people that we hunted a good hunt before we died.

"You will not try to follow me," Denikazi continued. "And should you see any signs of Eskimos you will abandon this camp as if the devil Wendigo was on your heels, and flee into the south."

When the chief and his five companions had left the camp, and their canoes were only tiny black spots on the distant water, Jamie spoke his mind to Awasin. "We promised we wouldn't follow him, but that doesn't mean we can't look for the deer on our own. Anyway *I'm* not going to sit here for six days just looking at those two Chipeweyans!"

It was very rarely that Awasin grew angry. This time he did. "Sometimes you chatter like a child!" he exclaimed. "You know nothing about this land, but Denikazi knows it well. You are like the weasel that climbed into the cookstove to see if it was hot, and got roasted for his trouble!"

Realizing that Awasin was seriously annoyed with him, Jamie changed the subject. But he did not change his mind. "Let's go for a little hunt," he suggested the next day, "not far — just to see if we can shoot some ducks."

Awasin accepted this idea and he explained it to the two Chipeweyans who had been left behind. They were young men, hardly in their twenties, disgusted at being left out of the deer hunt. They sat sullenly beside the fire and sulked.

But when the boys returned, the two Chipeweyans greeted them with enthusiasm. Jamie had shot two ptarmigan — arctic partridge — and Awasin a third. The Idthen men were hungry for fresh meat and the boys gave each a whole bird.

After the meal the four sat about the fire feeling well fed for the first time in many days. Telie-kwazie was rather a talkative man — for a Chipeweyan — and Awasin prodded him into telling a story.

Between sentences Awasin translated for Jamie, who was particularly interested in the legends about the country. Telie-kwazie told of a hunter who discovered the spirit Wendigo's trail in the snow. Jamie asked where this had taken place.

Telie-kwazie pointed up the Kazon. "I do not know for certain," he said, "but I have heard it was near the Great Stone House, a day's journey to the north."

"What is the Great Stone House?" Jamie immediately wanted to know.

"I have not seen it," Telie-kwazie replied, "but it is said that by the Kazon-dee-zee stands a house made of big stones. It is shaped like the wooden houses that the white men build, but it is much older than any white man. In ancient times it marked the boundary between our hunting lands and the country of the Eskimos. No one knows when it was built, or by what manner of men."

As the boys lay under their blankets that night, Jamie whispered, "Awasin! Let's go have a look at that stone house!"

Awasin had been half expecting this, and he was ready for it.

"No!" he said firmly. "If we go anywhere it will be back south when the six days are up. Forget about it."

Jamie sighed. "Oh well," he said, "maybe the deer will come tomorrow."

CHAPTER 6

No Man's Land

THE DEER DID NOT COME THE NEXT day, nor the day after. The boys put in long hours fishing but they caught nothing. They walked for miles over the plains, but they saw no more game. By the third day even Awasin was restless.

The two Chipeweyans went hunting during the afternoon and by suppertime had not yet returned to camp, so the boys ate alone. As the sun sank close to the horizon, Jamie drained his mug of tea, and spoke. "I'm going to check the nets. Maybe there'll be some fish for breakfast."

He strolled down to the canoe. With a quick movement he flipped it over and shoved it half into the water. Whistling casually, he put the paddles aboard and then, choosing a moment when Awasin wasn't looking, he hurriedly lifted two bundles that had been lying under the canoe, and stowed them aboard. Then with great nonchalance he picked up his rifle, climbed in and shoved the canoe out from the beach. He paddled a dozen feet, then let the canoe drift idly.

"I may be a while looking for the nets!" he shouted. "First I have to go and see about a stone house — down the river!"

Awasin dropped the tea-can, and came down the slope at a run. "Jamie!" he yelled. "Jamie, come back! You can't go down-river alone!"

Balancing the paddle on his knees, Jamie grinned. "I don't *want* to go alone," he said.

Awasin knew that he was beaten, and secretly he was rather glad. His desire to explore down-river had been almost as great as Jamie's, though tempered with caution and the knowledge that he was responsible for both of them. Now the decision was taken out of his hands.

"All right!" he shouted. "I'll go!"

Jamie laughed as he paddled to the beach. "I'll bet you want to go as much as I do!"

"Perhaps," Awasin said. He paused. "We must leave a message for the Chipeweyans."

44

There was a little square of rough sand near where the canoes were kept, and here Awasin drew an arrow in the sand pointed north. Beyond it he placed a tiny pile of little stones that vaguely looked like a house. Under the arrow he drew the universal symbol for two days' time — two suns with rays radiating from them. Then he climbed into the canoe.

Of all the great rivers that flow through the arctic, the Kazon is among the mightiest. Under its rolling surface there is a deep and unseen power that defies the puny strength of men. Coming down it from Kazba Lake, the boys had felt no fear of the river, for they had been traveling with men who know how to respect its power. Now they were alone, and in the shrinking twilight the great river had an awesome majesty. The water was black and heavy and the thrust of the current seemed to pass right through the canoe into the boys' bodies, so that they felt almost as if they were riding upon the back of some gigantic prehistoric monster.

The boys had no way of knowing for certain how far they had come from camp, nor how fast. The low banks slid past like shapeless masses of dark clouds. After what seemed like hours of tense waiting for the mood of the river to change, Jamie spoke. His voice was little more than a whisper, as if he were afraid to speak out loud in that murmuring silence. "We must have gone miles by now," he said softly. "How about making camp till morning?"

Awasin shook his head. "Not yet," he replied.

45

The canoe drifted on and the darkness became heavier. Then Awasin's straining ears caught the faintest warning sound. Faintly, so faintly it was hardly real, he heard the sound again and this time he recognized the menace of its warning.

"Rapid!" he shouted, and his shoulders hunched as he dug his paddle into the water and drove the canoe furiously toward the dim shadows of the bank. Jamie responded at once with the short, savage strokes used only in emergency. Seconds later the bow grated on the shore rocks and Jamie leaped out, knee-deep in the cold current, and dragged the canoe to safety on the bank. Awasin joined him, and together they made their way up to the level plains above.

The brief arctic night was already ending. The eastern sky glowed angrily and the few stars paled and disappeared. As the boys walked downstream an arctic fox flitted shadowlike from the rocks at their feet. They paid no attention to it. Their minds were filled with the rising roar of the rapid ahead. Even in the semidarkness of early dawn they could clearly see the broad expanse of shimmering whiteness where the waters, torn to fury by the unseen rocks, boiled up with a sullen, angry roar.

"It looks — pretty bad," Jamie said.

Awasin too was filled with uncertainty, but he would not show it. "Wait for the daylight," he said, "then we'll see."

They returned to the canoe for a brief nap, then waking, gathered a few handfuls of moss and willow twigs, and brewed up tea. Sipping the hot brew they watched the world awake.

The edge of the sun tipped a distant ridge and light flowed over the darkened plains like a flood of yellow metal. The sky faded from blood-red, through yellow, to a vivid green. A single goose beat heavily out of the grass-colored sky and its sad cry echoed over the wakening world. Flights of old squaw ducks got up hurriedly from tundra pools and winged off to the big lakes. It was morning.

The boys got stiffly to their feet and returned to their lookout point. A high bluff thrust its blunt nose out into the seething current. The river narrowed here, and for half a mile ran down a steep and rocky stairway, with the uncontrolled violence of a stampeding herd of buffalo.

Carefully they studied the rapid. At the top the oily waters drew in as if about to plunge down a huge funnel, and at this point there was the beginning of a channel. A narrow strip of racing current, a broken ribbon of dark water, twisted and twined down through the foam-capped waves and whirling eddies.

"There's the channel!" Jamie shouted above the roar.

Awasin was already following it with his eyes, carefully planning the course, and weighing up the chances of success.

"We could portage around it, Jamie, but we've run worse than this before, and it would be a hard carry over the muskeg. Suppose we run it. See that big black boulder halfway down? We'll have to double back against the current there, or else be carried over the next ledge."

"Okay," Jamie said. But despite himself, he shivered.

It was true they had run worse rapids before, but in the forest country, where a wrecked canoe probably meant nothing worse than a day's walk to the nearest Indian settlement. Here it was different. One miscalculation or one second's carelessness and they would be afoot (if they weren't drowned) on the unfamiliar Barrens, a hundred miles north of the forests. There could be *no* mistakes on the Kazon.

As they pushed off from shore Jamie felt a rising tension that almost made him sick. A moment later the bow of the canoe swung into the funnel's mouth. The unseen hand of the river grasped the canoe as a cat grasps a mouse. The banks began to fly past at fearful speed and the canoe dipped abruptly forward into the chaos of rock and water.

Kneeling with his legs braced against the canoe thwart, Jamie forgot everything except the wild thrill of the moment. It was like galloping bareback over a rocky slope. Dimly he heard Awasin's hoarse shout — "Here's the turn — *watch out!*" Jamie threw himself on his paddle and desperately tried to swing the bow of the canoe. A flying spume of spray engulfed the canoe so that he could see nothing of the fatal ledge ahead. Blindly he paddled, until it seemed his back would break. A rock rose suddenly out of the foam and touched the side of the canoe as lightly as a falling leaf touches the ground. The canoe

48

slithered sideways. Instantly Jamie drove his paddle between the rock and the canoe, and pulled back on the handle. The blade snapped off, soundlessly, and he almost fell overboard. As he struggled to regain his balance the fury of the river stopped abruptly, and the canoe floated gently in an untroubled backwater below the mighty rapid.

Still shaking with excitement, Jamie turned to look at Awasin. The Indian boy was laughing. He pointed to the broken paddle still clutched in Jamie's hand and shouted: "Were you trying to break the rock in half?"

Jamie grinned as he leaned back to pull the spare paddle out of the gear in the bottom of the canoe. "We made it just the same," he said. "Not even Denikazi could have done it better!"

Adroitly Awasin scooped up a paddle full of water and flicked it into Jamie's face. "Breaker-of-Rocks," he taunted. "That is your name from now on!"

The sun stood high by then and the morning was bright and clear. Leisurely the boys paddled down the river until they reached a broad stretch where the current sank away and disappeared. As they entered this "almost-lake" a flock of male fish ducks started up in panic and went skittering away across the water. The fish ducks could not fly, for this was the time of the midsummer molt and they had lost their flight feathers. Flapping their wings furiously, they pattered over the surface like little hydroplanes.

Jamie and Awasin were hungry and instantly took up

49

the pursuit. The birds stretched their long necks forward in terror, and redoubled their efforts to escape until they were actually running on the surface of the water.

When the canoe was almost upon the flock, every duck vanished as if at a given signal. Little ripples marked the dozen spots where the fish ducks had dived.

Quickly the boys headed back upstream, for they knew that fish ducks always prefer to swim against the current. They paddled hard. A minute passed, then ducks' heads began popping up like so many little periscopes. One was barely a yard from the canoe, and the duck was so surprised it dived at once without drawing breath.

Jamie caught a glimpse of its sleek, fishlike shape as the broad, webbed feet propelled the bird underwater like a small torpedo. He pointed with his paddle. Awasin swung the canoe in pursuit again, and when the duck surfaced a second time the canoe was almost on top of it.

The game — a grim one for the duck — went on for five more minutes until the bird became exhausted from lack of air. It lingered, gasping, on the surface a fraction of a second too long, and Jamie brought the blade of his paddle down expertly. A moment later he had pulled the dead duck out of the river.

"Good hunting," Awasin said. "Now for our breakfast."

Jamie was already busy plucking the bird as Awasin paddled the canoe to shore.

CHAPTER 7

The Rapid!

They landed on a stony point near a valley that cradled a sparse growth of dwarf willow scrub. Jamie soon had a fire going, and while he prepared the duck for cooking, Awasin walked inland to a low ridge from which he could get a look at the country ahead.

Off to the northeast he could see the looming bulk of the mountain they had seen from the Killing Place. Idthenseth — Deer Mountain. Awasin wondered if Denikazi was already hunting caribou under its distant slopes.

Awasin looked intently to the north along the line of the river, and he saw where it seemed to vanish in a maze of channels and little barren islands. There was no sign of human life. No smoke, no Eskimo kayaks. Feeling more at ease, Awasin made his way back to where Jamie had almost finished cooking breakfast.

After plucking and gutting the duck, Jamie had split it in half and spread-eagled the carcass on two sticks. Then he had thrust a third stick up through the duck crosswise, and planted the other end in the gravel so that the bird was held at a slant over the fire. The oil from the fat duck spluttered into the embers and sent up white flames and black smoke. The smell of roasting meat made Awasin's mouth water as he came close.

"Hurry up!" Jamie called to him. "It will be burned black if we don't eat soon."

"I wouldn't doubt it — with you cooking!" teased his friend. But all the same Awasin sank his teeth into his half of the duck with pleasure.

A flock of herring gulls came winging downstream, caught the smell of food, and wheeled overhead. Crying harshly, they settled into the water a stone's throw from the boys, and here they jostled each other furiously and shrieked out insults. Jamie flung them a duck bone and at once a battle began among the hungry gulls.

Awasin paid the gulls no attention. He was staring fixedly into the pale blue dome of the sky. Suddenly he jumped to his feet and pointed upward. "Look!" he shouted.

52

Startled, Jamie looked up into the hard brilliance of the sky, but he could see nothing except a distant wraith of clouds. "What is it?" he asked.

"Ravens!" Awasin answered. "The brothers of the deer. Look, Jamie, there must be dozens of them!"

Jamie at last picked out the tiny black dots, like specks of soot. The birds were so high up and so far away that they kept vanishing from sight.

"I see them," Jamie said. "But why get so excited about a few ravens?"

Awasin looked at him. "The ravens only fly in flocks like that when the deer are moving," he said. "A big flock of ravens leads every herd. That is why the Chipeweyans call them the deer's brothers. Probably the herds aren't more than twenty miles away right now."

It was Jamie's turn to grow excited. "Come on then," he shouted. "We'll meet them down the river!"

Jamie hurried to load the canoe and Awasin followed slowly. He stood on the shore for a moment, looking undecided and worried. "Listen, Jamie," he said, "don't you think it would be better if we headed back to the Killing Place? The deer will go by there soon and we could help Etzanni and Telie-kwazie make a hunt."

"No," Jamie answered stubbornly. "I'm going to see the deer, *and* the Stone House too!"

Awasin was deeply disturbed, but not for anything would he have admitted to Jamie that he was also a little frightened. Somewhere to the north, he knew, Eskimo eyes were probably watching that same flight of ravens and preparing for the hunt. It was obviously foolhardy to continue down the Kazon. Yet he could not bring himself to put his fears into words. Reluctantly he took his place in the stern of the canoe.

The little lake was soon crossed, and then a few miles of swift and violent river brought them to the maze of islets and channels Awasin had seen from the breakfast camp. There was little current here and the boys threaded their way among bare, rounded islands.

At length they emerged into another fairly narrow lake whose northern end was out of sight. Awasin anxiously scanned the shores ahead, seeking signs that other men — Eskimos — had passed this way. But all was still.

The day had swelled into a brilliant, cloudless morning with a cool south wind blowing over the plains. To the west, the shape of Deer Mountain loomed larger and closer, so that it did not seem more than ten or fifteen miles away. Jamie noticed this and commented: "If Denikazi had come down the Kazon he could have got to Deer Mountain in half the time."

Awasin let this remark pass. He knew that Denikazi had been wise. The boys were now deep into Eskimo country while Denikazi was safely to the west. "We are foolish to take the chance," Awasin thought. And in that moment he made up his mind that no matter what Jamie thought of him, he would see to it that they went no farther than the end of the lake on which they found themselves.

"If we don't find that Stone House by afternoon, we

turn back!" he said aloud. "We have come downstream fast enough, but going back will be another story. We'll be lucky if we *get* back in less than two days."

Jamie recognized the note of decision in Awasin's voice. He sighed and said, "I guess you're right. If we don't find the place by suppertime, we'll call it quits."

And then it seemed as if the Barrens themselves decided to play on Jamie's side. The south wind began to grow stronger and before long was strong enough to fill a sail. Jamie strung up a blanket on a paddle and the canoe fairly scudded down the lake. Even Awasin forgot his doubts in the exhilaration of flying before the rising wind.

Within an hour the boys could see the end where the lake narrowed sharply and once again became a river. Neither boy suggested taking down the sail. In fact the lake faded almost imperceptibly into the river and the current began so slowly and easily that the boys hardly noticed it. Filled with the enjoyment of the sail, they held their course around a projecting point of land.

As Awasin sent the canoe leaping around the point, Jamie, in the bow, gave a sudden cry of warning.

A scant hundred yards ahead, and stretching from bank to bank, was a wild cataract. The waters leaped downhill with vicious fury, curling and boiling over hundreds of sharp granite ledges that thrust up through the foam like the blades of knives. There was no channel anywhere to be seen in that chaos of rock and water. The whole world ahead was a roaring nightmare of destruction!

Sucked into the hungry current, the canoe was at the

edge of the abyss almost before the boys could catch their breath.

"The sail!" Awasin screamed.

Through the roar of water Jamie could not hear, but acting instinctively he was already struggling with the blanket. In his frenzy he lost his balance; the paddle-mast tipped overboard dragging the blanket with it. The water-logged blanket acted as an anchor and instantly began to swing the bow of the canoe around so that the boys were going down the rapid broadside on. Awasin frantically drove his paddle into the rocks in an effort to hold the stern until the bow could swing downstream again, but he could get no grip. The canoe swung more and more until it was completely broadside to the current and rushing furiously down upon the first granite ledge.

Jamie felt a sudden jarring blow and the next instant he was flung into the cataract. His head struck an exposed rock, and he knew nothing more for a long time.

Awasin was luckier. As the canoe crunched against the rocks like a matchbox under a hammer, Awasin managed to jump clear. He struggled for his very life against the suction of the undertow, and a few moments later he was flung over a ledge and down into an eddy where he bobbed about until he could regain his breath. Then the whirlpool carried him shoreward, flung him into a side current, and left him sprawling in the shallows of a back-water beside the bank. He was badly bruised and bleeding from a dozen deep rock cuts. But he was alive and conscious.

56

His first thought was for Jamie. Getting to his knees, he turned toward the thundering river and spotted Jamie floating face up in the backwater. Forcing his shaking legs to carry him, Awasin waded out, grasped Jamie by the hair and hauled him part way up the beach.

Driven by an instinct for self-preservation that not even the stunning suddenness of the accident could dull, Awasin turned back to where the shattered hulk of the canoe hung poised upon a fang of rock on the outer edge of the whirlpool. At any instant it might slip free and vanish into the rapids below. In it lay the only hope of life for them, and Awasin knew it. Waves of pain and nausea swept over him, but doggedly he once more waded into the water.

The current sucked at his trembling legs. He lost his balance as he reached for the canoe. One hand clutched the broken gunwale of the vessel, and he dragged himself up to it. From then on it was a struggle of sheer will power against the brute power of the river. In a daze he fought, inch by inch, toward the shore while the waterlogged canoe tugged and hauled away from him. Several times he lost his foothold and both he and the canoe swung back toward the fatal journey. Each time he managed to arrest the progress in the nick of time. At last he felt the canoe grate against the shore. Dizziness overwhelmed him. He stumbled forward on his knees — and fainted dead away.

CHAPTER 8

Alone in the Wilderness

HIGH ABOVE THE RAPIDS A HAWK soared over a darkening world.

Suddenly he folded his wings and came gliding downward in a plunging flight that ended barely a dozen yards above the churning surface of the rapid. With wings spread wide and tail expanded like a fan, the bird checked

58

his drop and sailed across the river. Curiously he stared down at two figures lying half on shore, and half in the water. They showed no sign of life, but the hawk nevertheless took alarm. Opening his hooked beak he screamed shrilly, then beat his way inland, gaining height until he became only a faint speck in the distant sky.

The cry of the hawk pierced to Jamie's mind through the haze of unconsciousness. He stirred. Shivering, he drew himself clear of the frigid water. A sharp spasm of pain shot through him as he drew his right leg up on shore. With sudden terror, he saw the roaring rapids and the smashed hulk of the canoe.

He tried to scramble to his feet but the pain in his leg was like a burning knife, and he fell back groaning.

"Awasin!" he cried frantically. "Awasin! Answer me!"

Hidden from Jamie by a ledge of rock, Awasin lay only a few feet away. Jamie's shouts roused him and he stood up dizzily. His head, bloody from a cut above the eye, appeared over the edge of the rock.

"What are you yelling for?" he asked almost peevishly.

Then he grinned, and limped stiffly around the rock to his friend's side. "You didn't think a rapid could drown *me*, did you?" he asked. "Why, I'm half fish. And you must be half muskrat — you were underwater long enough to grow webs between your toes! But the old canoe isn't going to swim any more."

The casual way he spoke, and the relief at seeing him still alive, raised Jamie's spirits. But the mention of the canoe brought him back to earth.

59

"What'll we do?" he asked anxiously. "I think maybe my leg's broken. It hurts like fury. And if the canoe's smashed, how'll we get out of this?"

Fear and hopelessness, combined with the pain in his leg, brought tears to his eyes.

Jamie, who had done the leading while all went well, and who had once taunted his friend with being frightened, was now the more frightened of the two. Awasin, the cautious one who had held back from Jamie's wild plans, seemed neither frightened nor particularly upset. His own life and the life of his people had always been filled with sudden and crushing accidents. And to survive these blows of fate the Crees had learned to waste no time worrying about what was past.

Awasin had already grasped the situation fully. The canoe was completely wrecked. They were at least forty miles from the Killing Place and perhaps much farther. This was Eskimo country, and a dangerous place to linger. Jamie was evidently unfit to travel on foot, and probably most of the gear in the canoe was lost. The situation could hardly have been any worse. But all Awasin was considering at the moment were the ways and means to make the best of things.

"Let's see your leg, Jamie," he said.

Painfully Jamie rolled up his trouser leg. Along his shin was an ugly purple bruise and the knee was badly swollen. Awasin felt the injured leg with tender fingers. At last he looked up. "I bet it hurts," he said smiling, "but it isn't broken. Only bruised. You will be able to run like a caribou in a week at least."

He put his hands under Jamie's arms and half dragged him to a more comfortable place where he could rest with his back against a rock. "You stay here," he said, "while I see what's left in the canoe."

As Jamie watched Awasin haul out the shattered canoe and start salvaging its contents, he began to feel a little better. He hoped Awasin had not noticed his tears. The matter-of-fact way Awasin went to work relieved some of the fear that had filled Jamie's heart and he made an effort to be of help. There was a pocket of driftwood near him — a handful of dry twigs — and he dragged himself to it and was about to light a fire when he realized he had no matches.

"Throw me the match bottle, Awasin," he called. "We'll have a mug of tea. That is, if there *is* any tea." It was a brave attempt at a joke — but it fell dreadfully flat when Awasin replied.

"No fire tonight. The grub box couldn't swim — and the matches were in the box."

Jamie's moment of bravery vanished. No fire and no food — these were blows too strong to bear. He gave way to a mood of self-pity.

"You'd better leave me and walk back by yourself," he said, and his face was working. "I got us into this. It's my fault. You'd better leave me here."

Awasin looked up in amazement.

"You must be crazy!" he replied. "Your head must have got a wallop too! Why would I leave you? In a day or two Etzanni and Telie-kwazie will probably come down the river looking for us. And if they don't, we will walk back to their camp. We can do it as soon as your leg is better."

Awasin turned brusquely back to his work. He began to sort out the pile of water-soaked gear. Only one rifle had survived, but there were almost a hundred shells for it. There was a hatchet, the tea-billy, a frying pan, blankets, some deerskin robes, a fishline, part of a fish net and some other oddments of camp equipment. One of the paddles, broken at the blade, had washed up on shore nearby. The tracking line, used for hauling the canoe up rapids, had remained tied to the bow thwart, and Awasin salvaged the fifty feet of half-inch rope.

As Awasin looked critically over the collection he felt almost confident. There was enough equipment here for any real woodsman to make a living with for several weeks at least.

Twilight was falling fast as Awasin gathered up the wet blankets and brought them up to Jamie.

"We're not so badly off," he said, and awkwardly patted his friend's shoulder. "But there's nothing much more we can do tonight. I'll bring up the front half of the canoe and we can use it for a shelter."

Half an hour later, when the two boys were huddled under the broken remnant of the canoe, Jamie relaxed a little. "Sorry I was such a chump," he muttered. A few minutes later both boys were asleep.

62

When Jamie woke in the morning he was alone. He crawled out from under the canoe and discovered that his leg no longer hurt so badly, though it was stiff and he could not use it. The sky was clear and the sun bright and hot. Jamie rolled up his pants and let the sun beat down on his injured leg.

Half an hour later Awasin came over the high bank carrying two animals the size of small ground hogs. Their fur was a brilliant yellow, unlike anything Jamie had ever seen before.

"What are *those* things?" he asked in astonishment.

"They are some kind of ground squirrel," Awasin replied briefly. "Like woodchucks, but they'll be good to eat. I'm hungry. How about you?"

Jamie grinned. "Sure. I can eat those queer-looking beasts if you can."

At dawn Awasin had left camp to scout out the land. He had gone less than half a mile when he spotted one of the brightly colored arctic ground squirrels sitting bolt upright on a ridge, whistling at him. Awasin had never before seen such a beast — but any animal was food just then. He had not brought the gun, and he was afraid to go back for it, so dropping on hands and knees he crawled carefully forward. When he was ten feet away he picked up a jagged chunk of rock and threw it with all his strength. It missed by an inch, and with sick disappointment Awasin saw the squirrel vanish down its hole.

He was about to turn away when a shrill whistle stopped him. The round head of the ground squirrel popped out of the hole again and the black beady eyes watched him curiously.

For a moment Awasin stared back while he racked his mind for a way of killing the beast. Then an idea came to him. Hurriedly he untied the moose-hide lacings of his moccasins. Knotted together, the two pieces stretched about six feet. He tied a noose in one end, walked up and laid the noose over the hole — down which the ground squirrel had vanished — went back to the end of the lacing and lay down.

Two minutes of tense silence passed, then the head popped up again. A sudden jerk on the moose-hide line, a moment's hectic scramble, and the animal was dead.

Flushed with success, he searched for and found another which he also snared. Then he started back to camp.

As he climbed a gravel ridge he saw a high hill a mile downstream. On its barren crest stood a square, ugly mass of stone. This could only be the Great Stone House that they had set out to find.

CHAPTER 9

The Kayaks on the Lake

THE GROUND SQUIRRELS WERE SOON skinned. They were plump and layered with fat. There remained the problem of cooking them, but lighting a fire without matches was not as impossible as Jamie feared.

Awasin went to work systematically. Using wood from the canoe, he cut a rounded stick about two feet long, and pointed it at both ends. Then he took from a canoe thwart a flat piece about six inches long, three inches wide, and an inch thick. In the center of this he carved a small coni-

65

cal cavity with his knife. Next he cut a small piece of cedar shaped rather like the segment of an orange, with another conical hole cut in one side. This was the "mouthpiece" of the fire drill he was making.

The final step was to take a three-foot length of rawhide and wind it two or three times around the pointed stick.

The fire drill was now complete and ready to operate. Placing the flat piece with the hole in it (the fire board) on the ground, Awasin inserted one end of his pointed stick (the drill) in the fire board's conical hole. Now he crouched over the drill, and taking the little mouthpiece firmly between his teeth, set it over the top end of his pointed stick. Then he grasped the two ends of the rawhide line and firmly, but quickly, began to spin the drill. The shaft spun rapidly, first one way, then the other, its two ends turning freely — one in the mouthpiece, and the other in the fire board.

Awasin pressed down hard on the mouthpiece and the friction between the shaft and the fire board increased. The wood grew hotter and hotter until a thin thread of smoke began to rise from the hole in the fire board.

Satisfied that the outfit would work, Awasin laid it down for the moment. After some searching he found a punky piece of willow root. With his knife he shredded this dry stuff into the hole in the fire board until it was almost full. Then he again set up the drill and made it spin at top speed. The spiral of smoke returned and in a few minutes the plug of shredded root was glowing hot.

66

Without stopping the drill, Awasin shouted through his clenched teeth: "Ge'm grath — quick Yamie!"

As fast as his injured leg would let him, Jamie gathered handfuls of grass and dumped it beside Awasin, who suddenly dropped the drill, picked up the fire board, and emptied the glowing shreds of root on the pile of dry grass. On his knees beside the pile, Awasin blew until his cheeks hurt. The smoke grew thicker until a tiny yellow flame leaped up.

The rest was easy. An hour later the boys sat beside the embers of their fire wiping the meat juices from their faces. Nothing remained of the ground squirrels except some well-picked bones.

Now that he was fed, and the fire problem had been beaten, Jamie was himself again. If it had not been for his aching knee he would have been almost ready to enjoy the adventure. "Awasin," he said suddenly, "I've been thinking. I can't walk on account of my leg, but maybe you should go back upstream a way and meet the Chips when they come looking for us. It'd be safer. They might not come this far otherwise."

Awasin nodded in agreement. "Yes," he said, "and if I go now I could walk to the other end of the lake by dark. But" — he paused and there was a note of uncertainty in his voice — "I might have to spend the night away from camp."

"You take the rifle then," Jamie said. "But what you're worrying about won't happen. You won't see any Eskimos."

An hour later, when Awasin had set off, Jamie felt very much alone. The faded sky above, and the endless roll of hills, gave him the feeling he was on a strange planet where no other human beings lived. The day was hot, but he shivered as he looked out over the wilderness of rock and moss. Then firmly he put the great loneliness out of his mind. To keep occupied he spent some time sorting and cleaning the gear salvaged from the canoe. After a while he looked up to find he had company after all. A pair of horned larks had come looking for scraps, and they scampered fearlessly about almost within Jamie's reach. Watching them, Jamie was aware that the feeling of absolute loneliness had vanished, and he was grateful to the little birds.

He had built up the coals of the fire for the third time when Awasin reappeared. Jamie glanced up to see a tiny figure running toward him. When Awasin was only a hundred feet away — and still running full tilt — Jamie felt his heart sink. Awasin looked terrified!

"Did you find them?" Jamie cried anxiously.

Awasin waved his hand frantically as if to say "Keep quiet!" — then he was beside Jamie, gasping for breath and panting. He jumped on the fire and scattered the precious coals furiously, tramping them out until not a thread of smoke still rose. Only then did he speak.

"Eskimos!" he panted. "Three boats full — out on the lake — we've got to hide!"

Awasin's fear was infectious. Despite himself, Jamie felt his heart pound furiously — not just from fear of the

Eskimos, but because it dawned on him immediately what the incident really meant. "That tears it!" he cried. "The Chips will never dare come looking for us now!" He stopped, horror-stricken at the thought.

But before he could dwell on it, Awasin, already at work packing the camp gear, paused to say, "Never mind that. We've got to hide, and quick! I think I know a place — the Stone House! The Eskimos are probably frightened of it. Come on!"

It took only a few minutes to roll their belongings into the blankets. Awasin shouldered the load and set off, while Jamie stumbled after him, half supporting himself with the broken paddle shaft.

They made painfully slow progress. Every few yards the pain would become too great to bear, and Jamie would have to rest. Fortunately their goal was only a mile away, but it was almost dusk before they staggered up the long hill and found a sheltered spot under the squat, black ruins of the Great Stone House.

Tired, hungry and frightened, they had no interest to spare then for the mysterious object that had brought them into their present trouble. Instead they wrapped themselves in the blankets and fell into an uneasy sleep.

In the meantime Jamie's fear about the Chipeweyans' giving up the search had been fully realized.

When Etzanni and Telie-kwazi returned to the Killing Place late at night and found the boys missing, they had been worried, and frightened as well. But the next morning, when they found the sign in the sand, Telie-kwazie and Etzanni were more angry than anything else.

"They went downstream!" Etzanni said furiously as he examined the marks in the sand. "They have been bitten with madness!"

Since Denikazi had made them responsible for the boys, there was nothing else to do but follow them. They launched their canoe and set out. "If we catch them in time they will have sore backs!" Etzanni swore grimly.

"And if we do not catch them, then the Eskimos will spill fresh blood," Telie-kwazie added.

Traveling slowly and with extreme caution, they had only reached the place where the boys had cooked the fish duck by the time night fell. Here they camped without fire. Tensely they kept watch through the dark hours, their rifles cocked and lying on their knees. Centuries of warfare with the Eskimos — of ambushes and dawn raids — were in their memories, and by morning they were two very frightened men.

It took all their courage to move on down-river, but they went. Before noon they came into the maze of channels, and at last emerged around a point to catch a glimpse of the long lake which ended at the fatal rapids under the Stone House.

The first glimpse the Indians had of the lake was also their last!

Desperately they spun their canoe around and made it fairly leap upstream again — for they had seen three slim kayaks putting out from shore only a mile or so ahead.

The missing boys were forgotten and so was everything else except the need to put as many miles as possible between themselves and the Eskimos. That very night, by superhuman effort, they regained the camp at the Killing Place. There they paused only long enough to collect the rest of their equipment. In the morning, exhausted from exertion and fear, they camped many miles south on the shore of Idthen-tua. The next day they made their way to the western arm of the lake, where they waited for Denikazi. There was no doubt in their minds about the fate of the two boys — to them, the boys were already dead.

Meanwhile, under the shadows of the Stone House ridge the boys were mercifully unaware that they had been given up as lost. And on the lake of the Kazon, three Eskimo hunters paddling their kayaks leisurely from point to point knew nothing of the panic they had caused, or of the presence in their land of strangers!

Awasin awakened first the following morning and, after a worried study of the river for signs of Eskimos, he turned to look at the surrounding plains. On all sides the Barrens were empty of motion and the only sound was the distant whistling of curlews. Nevertheless the fear of the Eskimos was still strong in his heart.

The Stone House stood on the crest of a long ridge that stretched westward and upward into a range of hills. On the skyline at the end of this range stood the massive shape of Deer Mountain, under whose western slopes Denikazi was at that moment probably preparing to meet the herds of caribou.

By the time Jamie wakened, the panic of the previous day had worn away. He had never really believed the tales of Eskimo ferocity, and this morning he felt foolish at having allowed himself to be so badly frightened. Also he was hungry, and his leg hurt with an angry and persistent pain.

"Well," he said, "whatever happens, we have to eat. What about it?"

Awasin shook off his nagging fears and rummaged through the pile of gear. He found the fishline — a strong one, with a heavy hook — but there was nothing he could use for bait. He thought a moment, then picked up one of the cardboard ammunition boxes. Carefully he tore off a strip of the blue-and-yellow paper and ran the hook through it several times so that it formed an S-shaped bait, hiding the barb.

"The trout may have begun their autumn run by now," he said, "and they will be as hungry as we are. Perhaps this outfit will fool them. I'll go down to the river and see."

Carrying the rifle, Awasin started off, and Jamie set about making a fire. He knew Awasin would not approve but, as he said to himself, "If any Eskimo does see the smoke, he'll probably run the other way faster than *we* ran yesterday! Anyway," he concluded his thought, "I'm not eating raw fish if *I* can help it!"

In the meantime Awasin had found a large whirlpool just below a rapid. Squatting on the bank, he tied a small stone to his line as a sinker. Then he whirled hook and

72

sinker and about five feet of line about his head like a lasso. He let go suddenly and the weighted hook shot halfway across the river drawing the line after it. Slowly Awasin pulled the hook back toward the shore.

Nothing happened. Anxiously Awasin repeated his throw. This time he had only drawn in a few feet when the line snapped taut. Quickly he took a turn around his hand; the tightly stretched line jerked so hard it cut into his skin. Bracing himself, he slowly, carefully, dragged the line in toward shore.

Something swirled near the surface of the river and Awasin caught a glimpse of an immense silver shape, so huge it was unbelievable. His eyes glistened with excitement, for Awasin knew he had hooked one of the monster trout who spend their lives in the deepest lakes and only venture up the rivers when the run is on.

The great fish lunged violently as it came into the shallows, and nearly pulled Awasin off his feet. He did not dare drag it any farther for fear the line would break. Hurriedly he looped the line about a boulder and without an instant's pause leaped into the swirling water.

He splashed into the river only inches from the giant fish, and it lunged viciously so that spray shot high into the air. The line hummed with the tension, then snapped suddenly. Awasin was ready for it. Both his hands were clenched in the red gills of the mighty trout!

The plunging, struggling fish knocked Awasin over on his back — but still the boy hung on. Shouting with excitement, he struggled to haul it into shallower water.

73

Then one of his hands lost its grip. Desperately he flung himself forward and the trout's broad tail smashed against his face.

With the quickness that can mean the difference between starvation or survival, Awasin acted. He sank his teeth into the trout's tail, and hung on like a terrier.

A few minutes later, soaked, and shaking with excitement, he had the fish in the shallows. He groped around with his free hand, found a rock, and with one heavy blow ended the fight. Then he dragged his prize up on the bank.

It was worth looking at. Four feet long, it would have tipped the scales at more than forty pounds. Its gleaming flanks were heavily speckled with crimson and gold. Its huge mouth was as big as a Husky dog's, and set with hundreds of sharp teeth.

Happily Awasin shouldered the big trout and carried it to camp. He was so pleased by his victory that all thoughts of danger had momentarily vanished from his mind and he did not even remark on the fire that Jamie had built — after an hour of trying.

Jamie stared incredulously at the giant fish, then snatching his knife began slicing off thick steaks of the pink, salmonlike meat. In a few minutes the morning air was heavy with the smell of roasting fish, and the boys began to stuff themselves.

When they were completely full they found that they had hardly made an impression on the pile of steaks Jamie had cut off.

74

"We must not waste it," Awasin said. "It may be a while before we have a catch like this again. We'll smoke and dry the rest of it."

Setting a number of flat stones on edge around the fire, the boys hung strips of trout over them. Then they piled wet moss on the coals, heedless of the smoke that rose straight into the pale sky. The heavy smoke curled around the fillets, and they began to darken and to dry.

As the boys sat watching, the words that neither one had wished to speak came unbidden to Jamie's lips.

"We'd better face it," he said quietly. "We're in a mess right to our necks. And through my fault. Telie-kwazie and Etzanni will never find us now — and we'll never find them either."

CHAPTER 10

The Great Stone House

THOUGH THE BOYS KNEW THAT NO Chipeweyans would dare come up the river while the Eskimos were about, the situation was not yet hopeless. Jamie's leg was better. The weather was still good, and it would be possible to travel across the plains on foot for another two or three weeks without serious difficulty. But which direction should they go?

The Killing Place would certainly be deserted by the time they could get through. And to attempt on foot the long journey all the way south to the forests was out of the question. There was only one alternative.

There was a strong probability that Denikazi was still in the vicinity of Idthen-seth for, even if he had met the deer, he would need several days to make his hunt and to dry the meat for transportation home. From the ridge by the Great Stone House the boys could clearly see the mountain called Idthen-seth, and they estimated it was not more than thirty miles away.

Sitting by the fire in gloomy silence, both Awasin and Jamie separately came to the conclusion that their only hope lay in traveling west to intercept Denikazi.

"Things may not be so bad," Awasin said. "I think we stand a chance of meeting Denikazi if we can get across to Frozen Lake River. It's high ground all the way, so we wouldn't have trouble crossing streams and muskegs as we would going south."

"It's the only thing we *can* do, I suppose," Jamie replied. "But if we get there too late . . ." He left the sentence unfinished.

"We won't!" Awasin reassured him. "Anyway, we can't wait here."

They discussed the plan in detail and decided that they would have to move as soon as they could, and at top speed. However, there was no use starting until Jamie's leg was a little better. In the meantime Awasin undertook to catch more trout so they would be sure of having food once they left the river.

Left alone at camp, Jamie limped about gathering twigs and moss for use in drying the fish. On one trip from the fireplace he came under the shadow of the stone structure on the ridge, and stopped to glance up at it.

His curiosity about the Great Stone House had died abruptly at the time of the accident. Until this moment he had deliberately ignored the massive stone ruin which had once been his goal, and which now lay close at hand.

Now he looked at it, looming mysteriously above him, and thought, "I came here to see you, and got in a mess doing it. I might as well take a good look while I'm here!"

Resolutely he limped to the crest of the ridge and stood staring at the ruins.

Whatever the structure had once been, it was now hardly more than a rough rectangle of rocks about fifteen feet square and ten feet high. Jamie was sure that no Eskimo or Indian would have constructed anything so massive and so regular in outline; but he was also sure that no white man had come this way before. "Funny," he thought as he hobbled closer, "it looks like a fort or a watchtower without any doors or windows."

He began to poke about among the moss-grown rocks at the base. Arctic hares had been using the crevices between the stones as hiding places, and as Jamie fumbled among the rocks one of the big hares leaped out almost at his feet and fled like a gray ghost. Jamie got to his feet and circled the building looking for an opening. But he found none. The whole thing seemed to be one solid mass of masonry.

Jamie began to think it was only a huge cairn, or monument, and not a building at all.

He went back to the place where the hare had jumped out and here he found a deep crevice in the rocks. He peered in, and what he saw made his heart beat faster.

The crevice led into a cave, and in the semidarkness Jamie saw the vague outline of something that was certainly not stone. He lowered himself to his knees and squeezed his head and shoulders through the opening.

His body blocked out the light but his outstretched hands touched something cold and rough. He gripped it, and backed out of the hole dragging the object with him.

As the sunlight fell upon it Jamie's eyes grew wide with wonder, for in his hand he held a sword! And what a sword it was. Four feet in length, it had a double-edged blade and a two-handed hilt. It was the sort of weapon that only a giant of a man could have handled. The blade was deeply pitted and rusted and on the hilt were broad rings of gold, turned greenish by centuries of weather.

Fascinated, Jamie hefted the heavy weapon, then he laid it down and crawled back into the hole. Again his hands touched something and he scrambled out, bringing with him a bowlike helmet of some metal that had resisted the attacks of rust. Two hornlike studs were fastened to the sides of the helmet.

Jamie had seen pictures of such a helmet as this in his schoolbooks, and he recognized it at once.

"This is the kind of helmet Eric the Red and Leif the

Lucky wore!" he whispered. "And that means — that the ancient Vikings must have built this place!"

Unable to contain his excitement, Jamie hobbled to the edge of the hill and began calling for Awasin.

Down by the riverbank the Indian boy heard the cries, and the ever-present fear of Eskimos returned. Grabbing the three trout he had caught, he raced full tilt up the long slope to the camp.

Jamie was not there! He dropped the fish and grabbed the rifle, then a scuffling noise from the crest above him made him turn.

Awasin was levelheaded, but this time he almost panicked. A huge, horned head, dull green in color, peered over the summit of the hill, and an unseen hand brandished a mighty weapon such as Awasin had never seen before in all his life. He raised the rifle with shaking hands and was on the point of firing blindly at the apparition. His finger tightened convulsively on the trigger.

Fortunately in that instant the spell was broken. Jamie caught his foot between two rocks, and fell. The helmet rolled away revealing his shock of blond hair and the sunburned face.

"Hey!" he yelled. "Help me up, you dope. And watch where you point that gun!"

A few minutes later Jamie was trying to explain his treasure find to a confused Awasin, who only vaguely understood what it was all about.

"It must have been like this," Jamie said, running his words together in his excitement — "hundreds of years ago some of the early Viking explorers must have wandered into Hudson Bay and then tried to come south up the Kazon. Maybe it was a thousand years ago. The Vikings came west from Greenland in open boats and some of them must have come through Davis Strait. This *proves* it!" Jamie continued. "I'll bet this sword and helmet are worth a thousand dollars to a museum!"

The thought of so much money left even Jamie breathless for a moment, and in the silence Awasin asked a question. The talk of Vikings and Greenland and museums was above his head, but one thing was clear to his practical mind.

"Perhaps you're right about all this," he said, "but just *how* do we get these things home?"

The question brought Jamie back to reality. "You *would* think of that!" he said bitterly. Then suddenly cheerful again: "Listen, Awasin. We'll leave the stuff right here, then next summer we'll come back and get it. Come on, let's see what else is in this old stone house!"

His enthusiasm restored, Jamie once more crawled into the crevice while Awasin, curious despite himself, stood ready to take the objects Jamie might hand out.

Worming his way downward, Jamie disappeared completely, but a few moments later his hand appeared. In it was clutched a dagger whose blade was rusted away to a thin sliver of metal. Awasin was examining it when Jamie's muffled voice called him back to the tunnel mouth. This time the object was a flat, square piece of gray metal about the size of an old-fashioned school slate. Its weight made

81

Awasin grunt in surprise. "This is made of lead!" he called to Jamie.

Jamie was busy tugging one more object out of the litter of fallen rocks and decayed moss. Finally he got it free and shoved it outside, calling at the same time, "What's this?"

For answer Awasin yelled as if he had seen a ghost. In fact he had. As he emerged into the daylight Jamie saw the object lying where Awasin had dropped it. It was a human skull.

Awasin was trembling. "That is a grave," he cried. "I'll take my chances with the Eskimos! We're moving camp!"

Jamie was in no mood to argue. Hurriedly he pushed the ancient weapons back into the crevice and rolled a rock over the entrance. The skull he left severely alone. Then he hastened after Awasin.

As he hobbled away he saw the small square of lead, and rather than go back to the grave again he picked it up and took it with him.

Already Awasin had the camp gear rolled in the blankets. He was stuffing dry fish, fresh fish, and partly dry fish into a bag he had made from an old deerskin robe. His dark face was tense and anxious. Awasin wanted nothing so much as to put many miles between himself and the white skull beside the Great Stone House.

They moved away a few moments later with Jamie limping badly and still using the paddle as a crutch. The sinking sun lay straight ahead, and its crimson rays fell full upon the ancient tomb whose history lay buried under the weight of a thousand winters.

As night fell they made a new camp on the long ridge that ran westward like a ramp toward the bulk of Idthenseth. After a skimpy meal of fish, Jamie sat silent for a little while staring curiously at the thin sheet of lead he had brought with him from the tomb. Awasin watched with disapproval, for to him it was an evil thing to carry away the possessions of the dead.

At last Jamie spoke. "It's covered with some kind of writing," he said wonderingly. "Queer-looking, like picture writing." He paused, looking back at the distant crest of the hill where the ruins stood. "I'll bet if we could read it, we'd know the story of those old Vikings at the Stone House."

Faintly illuminated by the last rays of the evening sun, the shape of the Great Stone House hung on the far horizon — a mystery still; but Jamie felt he held the key.

CHAPTER 11
Flight to the West

FOR THREE DAYS THEY CONTINUED westward toward Idthen-seth. The mountain grew steadily larger, looming like a gigantic frozen wave upon a motionless ocean of gray ridges.

As the days passed the boys became feverish with impatience, for the fear of missing Denikazi grew with each passing hour. They drove themselves mercilessly from dawn till dusk. At times, as they lay exhausted under their deerskin robes, they heard the whistle of unseen wings as flocks of sandpipers and plover passed overhead toward

84

the south. It was a sign that summer was near its end, and the boys longed to be able to join the high-flying birds on their journey south to safety.

By the end of the third day Jamie's leg had become so painful that he could not continue. Depressed by the delay, and miserable from weariness, the boys spent a silent day in a makeshift camp under the shadow of Idthen-seth. While they slept that night, the weather, so long their friend, turned enemy. Dawn on the fifth day found a dull and sullen sky with a cold wet wind whining down from the north. Awasin had trouble finding enough dry moss for a fire. As he watched his friend at work, Jamie's mood of depression reached its lowest point.

"We might as well give up," he said miserably.

At Jamie's remark, Awasin felt a weakening of his own resolve. He struggled to control his feelings, then he replied stubbornly: "We will get back all right. Lots of people have been in worse trouble than this and got out alive. We will be fine, if only the deer will come!"

He had been glancing hopefully out over the plains. Now he stiffened and jumped to his feet. For a long moment he stared intently into the somber distances. When he spoke his voice was vibrant with excitement.

"The deer *have* come!" he shouted.

Jamie looked quickly in the direction Awasin was pointing. Far off to the south a line of boulders crested a long ridge, and as the boys watched, those distant "boulders" shifted their position very slightly. They were not rocks — but deer!

Forgetting his injured leg, Jamie ran for the rifle. A sudden twinge brought him up with a grunt of agony. He turned to Awasin. "You'll have to hunt them alone," he said. "Think you can get one?"

Awasin grinned. "You watch." He buckled on the knife, picked up the rifle, and slid silently down the slopes toward the south.

The caribou were about two miles away and grazing slowly eastward. It was a small herd, perhaps a dozen beasts. The animals were wary and moved cautiously, stopping often to fling their heads up and stare suspiciously about them.

Jamie watched Awasin run lightly over a long muskeg, then eastward under the sheltering crest of a ridge. It was clear that Awasin was trying to get ahead of, and down wind from, the slowly moving deer. The country was open and offered little cover so he could not hope to stalk the beasts. Instead he had to pick a hiding place from which he could ambush the approaching deer.

When Awasin disappeared he was a mile ahead of the caribou herd, and from that moment Jamie could only watch the slow movement of the beasts, and pray that Awasin's judgment was good. Once the herd changed its direction and began drifting south. Jamie felt sick with disappointment, for he knew Awasin could not change position now without being seen. Then, aimlessly it seemed, the deer returned to their original route. The tension grew unbearable. Minutes dragged by and at last he heard the faint, flat sound of a rifle shot.

86

The tiny figures of the distant deer spread out as ants do when a man disturbs their nest. They were too far away for Jamie to see if any had fallen, but he trusted Awasin's marksmanship. Bustling about with no regard for his leg, he gathered more moss and heaped it on the fire.

When Awasin came back he was dog-tired but happy. Over his shoulder he carried the hindquarters of a fine young buck, and in his pack he had the tongue, kidneys, and back meat.

Fairly stuttering with excitement, Jamie grabbed the knife and began to hack off thick steaks. Draped by the side of the fire, the steaks soon began to give off a rich smell. Expertly Awasin sliced the deer tongue into thin pieces and set it to fry. The fat oozed out of it and sizzled merrily. Then he added the kidneys to the mixture. Finally he peeled the leg bones and thrust them into the heart of the fire, where the marrow soon began to spit and crack.

"It was easy, Jamie," he said. "I let them come so close they almost stepped on me. But the biggest news is that the plains beyond that ridge are covered with deer, hundreds of them. The trek must have started some days ago."

Jamie paused in the act of turning the steaks. "Maybe that's *not* so good," he said slowly. "If the deer reached Denikazi's camp two or three days ago, he may be ready to head back south again. We'll have to make speed to reach the river in time to catch him."

This sober thought rather took the wind out of Awasin's sails. But nothing could entirely take away the pleasure of a good meat dinner after days of fish. Before he dropped off to sleep, Awasin turned to Jamie. "Tomorrow we will reach the river," he said, "and catch Denikazi." Fully fed and content, Jamie was willing to believe his friend. The boys slept heavily that night despite a recurring dream that haunted Jamie — a dream of Denikazi paddling his canoe far to the south, without them.

The new day began well, with a clearing sky. And hurriedly the boys packed the rest of the deermeat in their homemade packs and set out.

As they moved across the south tongue of the mountain they could see the blue shadows of the distant range of hills which they knew must lie on the far side of the river they were seeking. Below them, on the wide plains, little herds of caribou drifted before the morning breeze. It was not the vast migration that they had heard about, but the presence of the deer, even in small herds, was a friendly thing that partially dispelled the loneliness of the Barrens.

As evening drew on, the weather turned foul, and a driving rain closed in about the boys so that they could no longer even see Idthen-seth, which was now to the north of them. They were forced to make an early camp, and a fireless one, for all the fuel was wet. During the long hours until darkness they sat impatiently, huddled close together for warmth. When they slept at last, it was a wet and miserable slumber broken often by the need to move around and restore their circulation. Sometime just after dawn, when a heavy mist still obscured the world about, Awasin could stand the strain no longer.

"Come on, Jamie," he said. "Let's try to find that river."

88

Breakfasting on cold scraps, they set out again, feeling their way cautiously over the rough ground. At length Awasin came to such a sudden stop that Jamie bumped into him. "Listen!" Awasin said. "Hear anything?"

Jamie strained his ears. Through the gray blanket of the mist he heard a faint muttering sound. For a moment he could not identify it, then he shouted. "Rapids! We must be near the river!"

Stumbling and falling over the half-seen rocks, they scrambled down a steep slope until they could see the dull sheen of running water. They had found a river, and it *must* be the river they were seeking.

"Let's walk upstream," Awasin suggested. "There are bound to be willows on the shore and we can build a fire and get dry."

A few hundred yards farther they found a clump of low dwarf willows, and in a little while they had a good fire roaring and fresh meat cooking.

"Even in this fog, they are sure to see our fire anyway," Awasin said. Jamie agreed. They were safe now, for sooner or later the canoes of Denikazi's party must appear on their way south. That night the boys slept contentedly, warm, dry, well fed, and secure in the belief that their ordeal was almost over.

They would not have slept so well had they known what was happening a few short miles away.

When Denikazi had set out with his hunters from the Killing Place, he had made his way up the west arm of Idthen-tua. Hardly pausing for rest, he had driven his men overland in search of the chain of portages leading to the River of the Frozen Lake. Five days after leaving the Killing Place, the hunters had still found no sign of the deer. Anxiously Denikazi had pushed forward to a place where the old Idthen Eldeli wanderers had often camped.

There was a fairly large lake at this point, and the hills rose up steeply on both sides of it. The foreshore was carpeted with the white bones of many thousands of deer that had fallen to the almost forgotten hunters of a century past. Most important, there was the remains of a "deer fence" here. This fence, built perhaps two hundred years earlier by Idthen Eldeli hunters, consisted of a line of stone pillars angling up from the lake to the slopes of the western hills. The pillars, each about three feet high, were spaced about thirty feet apart and they bore a remarkable resemblance to kneeling human figures. At a certain point in the line was a narrow gap, and on both sides of the gap hiding places of stone had been built for the Chipeweyan bowmen.

Denikazi knew of this deer trap from old stories, and so he decided to wait near it for the deer which must soon come.

He had not long to wait.

The great herds arrived a few days later — at the same time that Jamie and Awasin were making their way toward Idthen-seth.

In a few hours Denikazi's men had killed all the deer they could carry. The hearts of the Indians were glad,

90

for this great kill meant that the specter of starvation would soon be driven from the Idthen Eldeli camps by Kasmere Lake.

But there was no time to waste. Working by day and by night, the hunters cut up their kill and covered the dwarf bushes with thin slices of meat laid out to dry. In a few days the dry meat was ready to pack into deerskin bags. Then Denikazi began his dash for home.

Traveling despite the mist and rain, the Indians had come a day's journey from the lake of the slaughter, and on this night they were camped by the River of the Frozen Lake a scant ten miles downstream from the place where Awasin and Jamie were asleep.

It was well past midnight, and only one Indian was awake tending the fire. He had gone a few hundred feet from camp to collect more willow twigs when a slight sound made him glance up suspiciously.

The clouds that had obscured the moon dispersed, and a pallid white light poured down on the plains for a moment. In that brief instant the Indian saw a shape that made him stiffen with fear. He raced back to the sleeping camp calling a warning.

The camp woke to frenzied turmoil. The word "Eskimo" was on each man's lips, for the terrified Indians were certain that the enemy was about to attack them. The watcher by the fire had only glimpsed "something" that might have been the fur-clad figure of a man, but in the tense state of nerves that afflicted all the Indians in those weeks spent on the edge of Eskimo country, this was enough. Heedless of darkness or of rapids, the Chipeweyan canoes were flung into the river and went flying up the stream. The Indians paddled as if they were pursued by devils. Well before dawn their canoes slid silently past the place where two boys slept, beside the dead ashes of their fire.

CHAPTER 12

River of the Frozen Lake

AT DAWN THE BOYS SCRAMBLED out of their deerskin robes. A light breeze rolled in over the plains from the northwest carrying with it a faint barnyard smell. Jamie sniffed the air curiously, wondering where the smell came from. He climbed a hill near camp and looked across the river. There were the great herds at last! They were moving south in a never-ending stream in long, twisting lines, each deer following the one ahead. Thirty or forty of these strings — some of them two miles long —

were in sight at one time. They looked like giant brown snakes crossing a vast meadow.

From the river edge where he was getting water, Awasin called to his friend. "Come here!" he shouted. "I have something to show you!"

Jamie joined him, and Awasin pointed to the shoreline at his feet. Along it was a foot-wide band of whitish material that looked like a felt mat. It stretched out of sight, up and down the river, on both shores.

Jamie picked up a handful of the queer-looking stuff. "Why, this is deer hair!" he exclaimed.

Awasin grinned. "Do you think you could make a mattress of it?" he asked. "The old-time Chipeweyans used to."

"Where did it all come from?" Jamie wanted to know.

"From the deer. Right now they are shedding their summer coats and the hair is loose. Somewhere upstream from us the herds are crossing the river, and they shed so much loose hair that it makes this mat along the riverbank for miles and miles."

Jamie tried to imagine the numbers of deer that must be involved, but he found it beyond his power to estimate. That was not surprising. Down the valley of the River of the Frozen Lake more than a quarter of a million caribou were moving in the autumn flood toward the forests.

"Anyway it proves we must be on the right river," Jamie said at last. "There couldn't be more than one valley carrying so many deer. Shall we walk along the shore and see if we can find any signs of Denikazi?"

Taking only a small pack of meat, the boys set out up-

94

stream. For an hour they walked leisurely while on the opposite side of the river the endless flow of deer continued. Jamie noticed that they were mostly does and fawns and he asked Awasin about this.

"The does and fawns go first," Awasin explained. "They seem to get restless for the forests early. But the bucks are different. When the mating season comes along in October they won't have time to eat or rest for a whole month. So now they're still up north putting on fat to carry them through the fall. They won't start south for another couple of weeks —"

Jamie interrupted. "Look down there!" he shouted.

In a sheltered hollow by the riverbank below them was the unmistakable debris of a campsite. Wild with excitement, the boys scrambled down to what had been Denikazi's first camp on the river during his journey north. The boys found many signs to indicate that the camp was not very old, but what really filled them with joy was the discovery of a little cache containing some dry fish, some tea, and a little bag of flour. Obviously this food had been intended for the homeward journey, and the fact that it was still untouched seemed to prove that Denikazi was still somewhere to the north.

Actually Denikazi and his men had slipped past this cache the previous night in their panic-striken flight. With their heavy load of meat they had no real need to pick up the cache. At this moment the Idthen Eldeli men were already beginning the long chain of portages back into Idthen-tua Lake.

Much relieved, and quite certain that they would be picked up in a day or so, the boys returned to their camp and spent the rest of the day waiting, resting, and gorging on caribou meat. They relaxed for the first time since the awful moment on the rapids near Stone House. Jamie's leg benefited from the rest, and he found that he could again put his weight on it without pain.

At noon the next day the boys decided to go north and meet their rescuers along the shore.

The weather remained fair and they enjoyed the walk. Many birds were moving south. A flock of Canada geese rose from a tundra pond and beat heavily into the clear sky calling their haunting notes. Flocks of longspurs — little sparrowlike birds — rose in front of the boys like clouds of dust. Curlews and golden plover whistled and called from the riverbanks. Hundreds of family parties of ptarmigan cackled from the willow swales along the route. There was food in plenty, but the boys wasted no ammunition, for they still had enough deermeat to last a few days longer.

By evening, when they had found no further signs of the Indians, they began to feel distinctly uneasy. That night they slept fitfully. In the morning Jamie put their doubts into words.

"Do you think they might have gone home by a different route?" he asked suddenly.

"No," Awasin replied stoutly. "They must still be down-river from us. We will walk for another day. We should find their camp, or see their canoes before nighttime."

Impatience and worry made them hurry their pace. By late afternoon they had come in sight of a big lake. Knowing that the Idthen Eldeli hunters would have chosen the west shore where the deer were, the boys crossed the river at this point. The water was swift but not too deep and they managed to wade, and jump, across a shallow stretch. They had hardly climbed the opposite bank when they smelled a pungent odor.

"Something awful dead around here!" Jamie said, wrinkling his nose in disgust.

A short search showed them what it was. Behind a knoll lay a dead caribou that had obviously been shot. The find cheered the boys up amazingly.

Hurrying on, they made their way down the west shore of the lake in the last rays of the setting sun. Suddenly Awasin spotted a flicker of light far ahead. "Campfire!" he yelled.

Immediately, Jamie lifted the rifle and fired half a dozen signal shots. The sounds echoed off the hills on both sides of the river, but the signal went unanswered. Only a growing silence followed the dying away of the fusillade. Worst still, the distant flicker of light winked out and vanished.

The boys looked at each other in stunned silence.

"Maybe we scared them," Jamie said hopefully. "After all, they don't know we're here. Maybe they think it was Eskimos shooting, and put out their fire on purpose."

Both boys grasped at this explanation. There was no use trying to go farther that night and, if Jamie's idea was

97

correct, it might even be dangerous to blunder into the Idthen Eldeli party in darkness. So, not bothering to light a fire, the boys made camp and slept restlessly under their blankets.

When Jamie awoke, Awasin was standing on a rock straining his eyes toward the north for signs of smoke from the Indians' breakfast fires. There was no smoke. As far as the eye could see the long files of caribou moved unperturbedly down the valley. They saw all this with something near panic in their hearts. For they both knew that if there had been hunters to the north, the deer would have been disturbed.

"Come on," Jamie said, "never mind breakfast. Let's get going quick. If that *was* Denikazi's fire we saw last night, we should reach his camp by noon. And if it wasn't . . . well . . ." He did not finish the sentence. Already the terrible thought that they had somehow missed the Indians was becoming a certainty in the boys' hearts.

They pushed forward at top speed. Shortly before noon as they came opposite a cliff on the western hills, a sudden flash of light caught their eyes. There could be no doubt what it was. Up on the cliff a sheet of quartz, or mica, was catching the sun's rays and reflecting them like a bright mirror. With sinking hearts the boys understood that this must have been their "fire" of the evening before.

Fear mounted steadily in their hearts, but they pushed forward grimly. And in the early afternoon they came at last to the deer fence.

The gap was close to the lake shore, and the camp where

the Chipeweyans had made their kill was near at hand. It did not take the boys long to discover it, or to read the ominous message it held for them. The remains of many caribou told the story of a successful hunt — some days before.

With sinking hearts they searched for some sign that the Indians might have gone on farther north. There was no such sign. Instead there was clear evidence that the Idthen Eldeli had stayed at this place only long enough to kill and prepare many deer — enough to fill their canoes to overloading. Remembering the urgent need for meat at the home camps, the boys could hope no longer. They knew now beyond a doubt that the hunters had gone home!

Jamie's voice trembled when he spoke. "How could we have missed them, Awasin?" he cried. "How *could* we have?"

Awasin had no answer. He too was crushed by the knowledge that the rescue which had seemed so certain had now vanished utterly. He knew there was no hope that Denikazi would return even after he heard the boys were missing. If he searched for them at all it would be along the Kazon. They had made a gamble — now they knew that they had lost.

In order to avoid thinking about their desperate plight, Awasin busied himself lighting a fire from the heap of willows left behind by the Chipeweyans. Methodically he placed pieces of meat to cook before the flames. With the fatalism of his ancestors he refused to think about the mistakes which were past.

99

It was different with Jamie. The future was close to him, and terrifying. He knew that the nearest friends were three hundred miles away by canoe — and they had no canoe. Summer was coming to an end, and long before they could walk even a small part of the way home, winter would fall upon them and they would perish.

Jamie thought about his uncle, about Macnair Lake, and finally his restless thoughts came back to the Great Stone House — the cause of all the trouble. "It was my fault," he thought. "I got Awasin into this."

From his pocket he drew out the thin sheet of lead he had taken from the old Norse tomb. He was about to throw it away when something made him pause. His mood of depression seemed to lighten. Courage began to flow back into his heart, for he was thinking: "Those old Vikings — they sailed thousands of miles across the oceans in boats we wouldn't dare to use even on Reindeer Lake! And they explored right into the Barrenlands a thousand or more years ago. Something hardly any white man has done since. They weren't afraid of anything at all!"

Slowly he put the lead plate back in his pocket and stood up. He began to speak, and though his voice trembled a little he was in control of himself. Jamie Macnair was almost a man.

"We'd better face it, Awasin," he said. "There isn't a chance for us to get out of here alive before the winter comes. But if the Eskimos can live here all winter long, then so can we!"

Awasin smiled. Getting to his feet he shook himself, as

if to clear away the grim forebodings that had lain over him. "That's Cree talk, Jamie," he said. "Good talk! You are right. If we can get food and clothes and shelter we will be all right. We *can* get all those things if we really try. Then, in the winter, we can make a sled, load it with meat for the journey, and head for home, cross-country."

Awasin's dark eyes glittered at the prospect of the arrival back at the Cree camps. He could see it in his mind. They would not be boys any longer, but hardened adventurers with such a tale to tell that even the old men of the tribe would listen with awe.

Jamie caught the enthusiasm in Awasin's voice and he began to feel the challenge of the adventure. "We'll trap white foxes," he said excitedly. "When we get back we'll be rich as well as famous."

Ignoring the difficulties they would have to face, they squatted by the fire and talked. Plans were made, discarded, and made again. They talked until they were exhausted. Then the excitement drained away and the immense and lonely arctic plains closed in upon them once more. All the cheerful talk seemed now to be only dream-stuff.

The fire flared up brightly, and in the sudden spurt of light Awasin and Jamie looked at each other with intent eyes.

Suddenly Jamie jumped to his feet. "All right!" he said loudly. "We've made our brag. Now let's live up to it!"

CHAPTER 13

Plans and Preparations

By MORNING THE FIRST SHOCK OF
their predicament had worn away and the boys were ready
to meet reality. No amount of brave talk could hide the
fact that they were faced with many months of living in
one of the most inhospitable places in the world — and
with nothing to help them except their wits and a piti-
fully small array of tools and weapons.

In order to survive at all they would have to stay in one
place and devote all their energy to building up supplies
of food, fuel, and caribou hides for clothing and for shelter. On foot, and ill-equipped, any attempt to break out to
the south was doomed, for winter was almost due. When

the snows came the Barrens would be indeed barren of food and shelter both.

Luckily the day broke clear and warm. The great plains looked almost friendly, and under the influence of the driving herds of deer, and the noisy movement of the birds, the boys managed to keep their spirits up and to begin their preparations.

The first task was to take stock of what they owned. There was the rifle, and ninety shells for it. There was a short hatchet, a long hunting knife, two smaller pocket-knives, a strong fishline with a single hook, a length of gill net, a file, the paddle Jamie had used for a crutch, fifty feet of half-inch rope, a tin tea-billy, an old frying pan, the fire drill Awasin had made, the lead sheet from the Norse grave, and about ten pounds of dried fish and fresh deer-meat. In addition there were their worn blankets, and the clothes the boys were wearing. Their rubbers and moc-casins were almost ruined by the long trek overland, and their trousers and jackets were thin and torn in many places.

All in all, it was not a very impressive outfit, but Awasin was cheerful. "It may not be all we want," he said, "but with this to start with, we can *get* everything we need from the country. We can kill deer — and deer can give us a lot more things than food and clothing."

Jamie glanced over his shoulder toward the gap in the deer fence, through which a steady stream of does and fawns was moving. "Hadn't we better start shooting then?" he asked anxiously. "Maybe the deer will be gone soon."

Jamie's anxiety was natural. It seemed impossible that such numbers of caribou could continue moving out of the north for much longer. And it was clear that the caribou were the key to life itself, as far as the boys were concerned.

Awasin shook his head. Then he explained why there was no great hurry to slaughter deer. In the first place it would be much harder to preserve the meat now than it would be if they waited until cold weather came and the meat could be frozen. Even more important was the fact that the great bucks — which were still to come — were far more valuable than does. The hide of the bucks was tougher and better for many things, and the bucks were fatter. This was vitally important, for a great deal of fat must be eaten by anyone who tries to survive a northern winter on a strictly meat diet. Fat could also be burned in crude lamps, and in a land where the winter night is long some kind of light is essential.

Awasin's idea was that they should shoot only a few deer at the moment, and save the precious ammunition till the migration of the bucks was at its height. Somewhat uneasily Jamie agreed to wait; then another question occurred to him.

"What'll we do about wood to burn?" he asked.

This time Awasin was at a loss. It was clear that once the snows came, it would be nearly impossible to gather enough dwarf willow scrub for cooking, let alone for heat-ing. And there appeared to be no other kind of wood about.

At last Awasin said, "Let us not fret about wood until we can think of an answer. Let's take one problem at a time."

"Well, then," Jamie said, "I guess we need some kind of shelter first; then enough food to last until the bucks arrive, and maybe enough skins for some kind of clothing. It won't be too long before the frosts hit us."

Awasin stood up and took hold of the rifle. "The deer will give us all three things," he answered. "Let's go hunting."

The boys walked along the line of stone pillars until they reached the gap. The deer saw them approach and veered off uneasily to mill about some distance from the fence. They were not seriously frightened, though, and they were very anxious to pass the fence and continue on their journey south.

The boys slid into a hiding place made of stones piled in a circle near the mouth of the gap, and crouched out of sight. There was no wind to carry their scent to the deer, and in a few moments the herds began to press forward again. The leaders came cautiously, stepping high and holding their nostrils up as they took great snorting breaths to test the air for danger.

"We won't shoot for a while," Awasin whispered as the deer came close. "Let them forget about us, then we can pick the herd we want."

An old doe followed by two fawns braved the gap and

105

galloped off toward the south. Behind her, small herds began to follow. In a few minutes the flow was steady again.

Jamie began counting the numbers that passed, but when he reached a thousand, he gave up. "I never thought there were that many deer in the whole world!" he whispered. Awasin did not reply. Instead he squeezed Jamie's arm and nodded toward a compact herd of about sixty animals slowly approaching. These were mostly young does, and they looked fat and sleek. A few fawns grunted about behind their mothers, or made short dashes ahead of the herd.

"That is the herd!" Awasin muttered. "I'll do the shooting, and you be ready to kill the cripples when I stop!"

Tense with excitement, Jamie at the same time felt a sensation of revolt against killing the approaching deer. They were so tame, so magnificent, and so very much alive that he hated the prospect of the slaughter. "Do we have to kill the does?" he whispered urgently. "What'll happen to their fawns?"

"Forget about it," Awasin replied shortly. "I hate it as much as you do. But the fawns will be all right. They're old enough to be on their own by now."

There was no further time for argument. The herd was bunching into the gap. Awasin knelt forward, rested the rifle on a lip of rock and opened fire. Shooting quickly but skillfully, he dropped the two leading beasts; then, half turning, he shot three more animals in the rear of the herd. The deer in the center reared and snorted in sudden

106

fright but did not break away, for they were blocked by the dead bodies ahead and behind. Some stood stupidly in one spot, gazing about with their large eyes for some indication of the danger. They did not understand what was happening until the smell of fresh blood struck their nostrils. Then they stampeded — but it was too late. Methodically, quickly, the rifle cracked. When the herd broke free of the deathtrap, nine of their number lay upon the rocky ground, and three fawns ran foolishly about beside the bodies.

Awasin put down his rifle and turned away. Jamie knew how Awasin felt. For this was slaughter. It was like shooting cows in a barnyard, Jamie thought. He was very glad Awasin had not asked him to do the killing.

Taking a deep breath, Jamie drew the long knife and walked over to the bodies of the deer. Only because it was absolutely necessary could he nerve himself for the task in hand. Fortunately all the deer were dead, and he had no need to finish them off. But he had to draw and skin them. Clumsily he set to work, and as he was struggling with the messy job one fawn came up close, grunting anxiously. Jamie tried to frighten it away. It would not go, but stood with its forelegs apart, sniffing at Jamie's clothes. He tried to ignore it and went on with his task.

Awasin joined him, and without a word began to help. Deftly and almost mechanically the Indian boy skinned off the hides and then cut up the meat. The hindquarters and forequarters he placed in one pile. In another went the tenderloins, the strips of tender back meat with their pre-

107

cious bands of sinew still attached, and the tongues. Hearts, kidneys, and livers went in still another pile with the briskets.

Not a thing was wasted. Having been forced to kill these does, Awasin was making certain that every ounce of meat would be used. Within two hours the work was done.

Only then did he speak. "All right," he said. "Now let's get this back to camp."

Jamie wiped his knife on the moss. "What about the carcasses and the scraps?" he said. "If we leave them here, they'll scare off all the other deer."

"Don't worry about that," Awasin replied. "Look overhead!"

Jamie had not noticed the arrival of hundreds of herring gulls. The big white birds swooped low above the gap, circling hungrily and filling the air with their raucous cries. "You mean *they'll* clean up for us?" Jamie asked in surprise.

"Wait and see," Awasin replied briefly.

He spread the fresh hides, weighed down with rocks, over the meat piles after he and Jamie had loaded all they could carry on their backs. At a jog trot they headed back to the camp, dumped their loads and returned. They had been gone no more than ten minutes, but when they reached the killing place Jamie saw with astonishment and disgust that each deer carcass had disappeared under a heaving, fighting, flapping blanket of gulls. Despite himself he shuddered. Quickly he shouldered another load.

As he set off now, the fawn came running up. Ungainly

108

and awkward, it scampered along behind him and made Jamie feel even more guilty about the slaughter of the does. Awasin was unloading at the camp when the fawn suddenly ran to him and nuzzled its nose against his legs. The Indian boy had not seen it, and with a startled shout he jumped halfway across the camp.

Jamie chuckled. "Looks like you've found a friend," he said.

Awasin grinned sheepishly. "I suppose since I killed its mother I have to be its foster father now," he replied.

"It'll probably wander away and join some other herd," said Jamie. "And if it doesn't maybe we can train it to draw a sled the way the Laplanders do with reindeer."

The fawn refused to wander. When the boys finished carrying all the meat and hides to the camp, it was still with them.

Now began the work of preparing the meat. Squatting side by side, the boys began slicing it into thin, waferlike pieces. It was tricky work, but Awasin was an expert. He went at the job as if he were peeling an apple, and gradually peeled the bigger pieces down to the bone at the core. When a large pile was sliced, Jamie picked it up and carefully hung the pieces above the ground on the branches of the scrubby willows. Under the bright sun, the meat began to dry at once.

Next Awasin turned to the hides. Choosing a sandy, level area, he stretched the skins, then pegged them down around the edges with the flesh side uppermost. Then he carefully scraped away the last fragments of tissue with the rounded end of his knife blade. The skin was of a bluish color, and Awasin remarked that it was not yet "prime" and not much good for clothing. "But it'll do for a tent," he said.

The next job was to strip away the three-inch-wide band of sinews that ran down the full length of each strip of back meat. These sheets of sinew, each three feet long, were hung to dry on the paddle, which had been stuck on end in the sand. At the lower end of each sheet Awasin tied a stone so that the sinew would dry straight. "Woman's work this," he complained to Jamie. "But we're going to need sinew thread before too long."

By dusk the jobs were finished. The boys were tired, but strangely content. After a good dinner they lay down in a makeshift tent they had erected, using stones, twigs, and "green" hides.

Their first day as dwellers in the plains had ended, and they had much to show for it. Nine skins; enough meat to make a hundred pounds of "jerky," or dry meat; supplies of sinew thread and plenty of fresh meat for daily use. Also, they had acquired a friend.

The fawn pushed its way under the edge of the tent to lie down awkwardly beside Awasin. Jamie pulled a handful of sedge and gave it to the little deer, who munched away contentedly.

Jamie stretched out on his blanket and sighed. "Not so bad," he said a trifle smugly.

"Don't be too proud. We still have much to do," Awasin answered cautiously.

110

CHAPTER 14

Camp at the Deer Fence

DURING THE NEXT WEEK THE BOYS found so many urgent jobs that they had little time for worrying. The weather was changing, and there was clear indication that summer days were done. There was heavy frost almost every night, and in the morning half an inch of ice lay on the tundra pools until the noonday sun melted it away.

Luckily the sun was still bright, and in three days the meat laid out on the willow scrub had dried. Jamie collected it carefully and packed it away in rough bags made from some of the "green," or untreated, caribou hides.

The main problem now was to keep warm. The make-shift tent, supported only by low scrub, was full of gaps. Their clothing was thin and their footgear almost worn out. After one particularly miserable night when they lay sleepless and shivering in their tent, Jamie decided to do something about the shelter problem. "We'll have to build some kind of house, Awasin," he said. "Maybe we could make a sort of igloo out of rocks. If we stuffed all the chinks with moss and covered the whole thing with deer hides it ought to be fairly warm."

"We must do something!" replied Awasin, still shivering from the night's chill. "You go ahead on the house. I'll see what I can do about some clothes."

Jamie set about housebuilding. There were plenty of flat rocks nearby and he gathered a pile of these at a spot beside the fire. Then he marked out a circle on the sand about five feet in diameter. Using the broad forehead antler from an old caribou skull, he dug out the sand inside the circle until he came to solid rock about a foot below the ground level. Next he began a circular wall, laying flat stones one on top of the other. At one point he placed a long, narrow stone across two others set upright in the wall. This was to be the door — a low, narrow entrance through which a boy, on hands and knees, could crawl.

It was ticklish work. Since there was no mortar to hold the stones, they had a tendency to topple inward and knock the whole thing down. When the wall was three feet high, it became so tottery that Jamie did not dare build it any higher.

112

His next problem was a roof. After much thought he placed the broken paddle across the top, like a rafter. Then he gathered armfuls of the longest willows he could find, and made a crude thatch that rested on the rock wall and on the shaft of the paddle. Over this he stretched a number of fresh caribou hides, with the fur side down. He arranged the skins in such a way that they sloped out toward the edge of the wall, so they would carry off the rain and melting snow.

His next task was to gather sphagnum moss and chink the many gaps in the wall. Then he hauled several loads of moss through the door and spread the spongy stuff on the floor as a kind of mattress. The house was done.

It did not look like much — in fact, from the outside it looked like another pile of rocks in a rocky world. But inside it was fairly snug and warm, and when Jamie hung a piece of deer hide over the doorway the little stone igloo was almost comfortable, even though there was no room to stretch out or stand up.

Meanwhile, Awasin had been hard at work trying to improvise new moccasins. Though he had often seen his mother and other Cree women making footgear, he had never before tried his hand at it.

He went at the job doggedly, determined to do well. The first task was to prepare the hide, and this he did by choosing three of the best deerskins and sinking them in a tundra pool, where he left them for two days. At the end of this time the hair had loosened and he was able to scrape it off with the blade of his knife. Next he cut out the leg sections of the hides, and the piece of skin which covers the caribou's forehead. These pieces were yellow, almost transparent when wet, and looked rather like parchment.

Awasin knew that the skin should be tanned, but this was a long and difficult business and he did not feel confident of success, so he decided simply to smoke the hides instead. He hung the skins over a fire smothered with wet moss, and every now and then he moistened the hides with water. After several hours the skins had turned to a dirty brown color, and Awasin judged they were ready to use.

Cutting the moccasins was easy. He took one of his own tattered moose-hide moccasins, slit the seams, and laid it out flat on the deer hide as a pattern. Some careful work with the knife gave him the rough material, cut out to shape. The Cree moccasin is designed in such a way that almost the whole thing can be cut from a single piece of hide. Then the seams are sewn together. It is not really difficult — with needles and thread. Awasin had neither, but like all those who live in the far north, he planned to make what he did not have.

He searched through the deer bones near camp until he found the shoulder blade of a young deer that had been killed by Denikazi's hunters. The flat center section was only about an eighth of an inch thick, and from this section Awasin chopped out a piece about as big as a playing card — and almost as thin. Then, using his knife as a splitting tool, and a stone as a hammer, he carefully sliced the bone into a number of slivers. They were the size of toothpicks. Sharp at one end, they were flexible enough to be

114

bent double without breaking. But they had no holes for the thread.

Awasin considered the problem for a while, and then he got the fishhook. Using the sharp point, he scraped away at the thick ends of his needles until he had made small holes right through the bone. He ruined half his needle supply in the process, but he ended up with five bone needles that — despite their thickness — looked serviceable.

The thread problem was simpler. Taking down one of the hanks of sinew, Awasin soaked this bone-hard strip in warm water for a few minutes until it became as soft and pliable as silk. Then, with his knife, he split off single threads, each about three feet long.

Now he was ready for work upon the moccasins. First using the fishhook to make the holes, he began sewing up the seams. At first his stitches were clumsy and too far apart, but Awasin was clever with his hands and soon he did a neater job.

He had used the leg hide of the caribou for the moccasins, since this is tougher and more durable than the body hide. All the same, the soles were thin, for caribou skin is not nearly so thick or tough as the moose hide which the Crees normally use. Awasin solved this problem by cutting extra soles from the very tough hide found on the forehead of the deer, and he sewed these to the bottom of each moccasin.

The finished moccasins were not things of beauty, but they would do. Jamie laughed when he saw them, but he was glad enough to pull on a pair in place of the tattered footgear he had been wearing.

The boys' socks had long ago been worn through, but by placing layers of soft grasses in the bottom of each moccasin they found they could keep their feet warm and comfortable. There was only one serious drawback. Being made of untanned hide, the moccasins would dry as hard as cardboard when they were not being worn. So each morning the boys had to fill them with water for a while before pulling them on. They were cold and clammy at first, but soon warmed up, and — better still — they were almost watertight.

His success with the moccasins encouraged Awasin to try making winter parkas. He had no good hides for this purpose, so he and Jamie agreed to use the two blankets they had brought with them. But Awasin soon found that a tailor's task is much more difficult than it looks. In the end he had to content himself with two capelike garments that could be pulled over the back and around the chest, but that had no arms. For the moment they would do. But when winter came, Awasin knew he would have to tackle the problem again.

By the time they had been a week in the camp by the deer fence, the boys had accomplished minor miracles. Not only had they provided themselves with the essential things they needed, but the very acts of building, and making, had filled them with a new self-confidence. They looked over their achievements with real pride. There was the "house"; there were moccasins, coats, and a hundred pounds of dry deermeat that would keep indefinitely and was equal to five hundred pounds of fresh meat. It was a lot of meat, but as Jamie looked at it the thought struck him that the winter meals were going to be monotonous.

"How about catching some fish?" he suggested one day. "When I was getting water this morning at the lake I saw plenty of grayling running. If we could just figure some way to set our net we could catch all we need."

Of course they had fished with nets before, but always from canoes. Setting a net from the shore is a very different proposition.

Their net was thirty feet long and four feet deep. Wooden floats were attached to one edge, and small lead weights to the other. Once in deep water it would float in an up-and-down position — but getting it into deep water without the use of a boat would be difficult.

"We can't set it in the lake," Awasin said, "but we might find some way to use it on the river. Let's walk down and see."

Carrying the net, the fishline, and the fifty-foot length of light rope, they set off along the shore of the lake to the point where the river began. It was half an hour's walk to the river mouth. Here they found a rapid, and just below it a tiny bay that had been cut into the bank by an eddy of the current. As they looked down into its cold, clear waters they could see the silvery shapes of lake trout, and the flickering shadows that were fat arctic whitefish.

"If we could just stretch the net across this bay we'd

117

catch all the fish we could use," said Jamie wistfully. Then an idea struck him. "Hey!" he yelled. "Get out the fishline!"

Awasin produced the line from his carrying bag.

"You stand on this point of land," Jamie ordered, "and I'll go round to the point on the other side of the bay, with the fishline. I'll tie a rock to one end and heave it over to you. Then you tie the rope to your end, and I'll haul the rope back so that it stretches right across. Then all we have to do is tie one end of the rope to the net, heave away, and we'll have it set in the mouth of the bay!"

Awasin was enthusiastic. "Go on!" he cried. "Let's see how it works!"

Jamie raced around the tiny bay to the far point, where he picked up an apple-sized rock and tied it to one end of the line. It was an easy throw, and the rock splashed into the water at Awasin's feet. Quickly he grasped it, took off the rock, and attached an end of the light rope. "All right!" he yelled.

Jamie began drawing the line across, and as the rope paid out at Awasin's end he made ready to fasten the net to it. At last the net itself began to move into the water and in a few moments it was set across the mouth of the little bay and anchored to shore at both ends.

Walking back to join Awasin, Jamie looked proudly out over the swirling waters where the line of the submerged net could be dimly seen.

Lazily the boys relaxed on the soft moss beside the river and enjoyed the warmth of the sun. Below them on the

118

rapids, hundreds of fish fought their way upstream, splashing and struggling to climb the waterfall.

"Even the fish are going south," Jamie said a little sadly.

"But not for long," Awasin answered cheerfully. "They only go upstream to spawn. In a few weeks they'll head north again to the Great Frozen Lake to spend the winter deep down under the ice. And if fish can spend the winter out here — we can too. Come on, let's see what we've caught."

Jamie ran around and untied his end, then he rejoined Awasin. Together the boys pulled the net into the shallows, and their excitement rose to fever pitch as they caught glimpses of great silvery shapes twisting and fighting in the net. The surge of the struggling fish yanked the net sideways and it took their full strength to drag it in.

"Look at that one!" Jamie yelled in wild excitement. "Looks like a whale!"

The first fish to lie flapping and leaping in the shallows was a monster, a lake trout almost five feet long. Its great mouth gaped and shut with a ferocious click and its rows of needlelike teeth sheared through the net as if it had been a spider web. Expertly Awasin leaped into the shallows and killed the giant with one blow on its head.

When the net was finally pulled out it held so many fish that it took an hour to untangle them all. Laid out on the moss, they made an imposing sight. There were fifteen lake trout, ranging from two to five feet in length. There were two dozen grayling — a kind of arctic trout — each about three or four pounds in weight. Most important of

119

all, there were thirty-seven plump whitefish, the king of all arctic fish when it comes to filling human stomachs.

Jamie's mouth watered with anticipation as he and Awasin cleaned and cut up their catch. Then, having piled rocks over what they could not carry, they shouldered a full load and set out for home.

As the crisp night air fell over the camp, it carried away with it the rich smell of frying whitefish. Beside the fire the two boys lay in complete contentment. Jamie sighed and said, "The way I feel right now I could live out here forever, and love it too!"

Awasin smiled. "The Crees used to say: Courage comes not from a strong heart, but from a full stomach! So we should be pretty brave!" He was silent for a moment. "We'll need all the courage we can find," he added. Awasin was staring out over the darkening plains, and he was no longer smiling.

CHAPTER 15

The Hidden Valley

ONE MORNING WHEN THE BOYS crawled out of their little stone igloo they found a faint powdering of snow upon the ground. The snow brought home the problem they had been trying not to think about. Winter was nearly here — and the question of fuel had yet to be answered. They had been able to gather only enough willow twigs for each day's needs, and they

121

knew that soon the low places where the willows grew would be filled with hard-packed drifts of snow.

Because they had been unable to solve the difficulty, they had tried to put it out of mind and had concentrated instead on the food supply. The net had yielded them a good quantity of fish and these had been prepared for winter use. Most of the whitefish and the smaller trout had been cleaned, split, and hung to dry over smoky fires of moss and green willow. But Jamie had hit upon a different plan to preserve the bigger fish. One day when he was digging out moss in a thick sphagnum bog not far from camp, he had come suddenly on solid ice. When he had cleared the moss away he discovered that there was a broad vein of pure ice — like a frozen stream — a few feet below ground level. This was in fact a frozen river. In very ancient times a stream had flowed through this bog and — perhaps during the time of the glaciers — had frozen solidly. It never had a chance to thaw. As the glaciers retreated, new moss grew across the *top* of the river, died, and was replaced with still newer growth. In time the frozen stream was buried under two feet of sphagnum moss, which is one of the best insulators in the world. No summer heat could reach the dead river, doomed to lie hidden and still forever.

Jamie was quick to see a use for the ice sheet. Together he and Awasin chopped a trench deep into the ice with the little hatchet. Into this trench they piled the cleaned bodies of the bigger trout, then covered them with moss. Within a day the fish were frozen solidly, so that it was al-

122

most as if the boys had a freezing machine right at the camp.

The frozen fish were later put in deep holes in the moss and covered over to keep until they were needed. Jamie thought the moss alone would be enough protection, but Awasin explained that there would be many other hungry stomachs in the plains that winter — many robbers who would soon scent the fish cache and try to get at it. "Omeenachee — the wolverine —will be our worst enemy when winter comes," Awasin explained. "Trappers call him the Glutton and he's a clever thief. If he gets into our food caches he'll eat, or ruin, everything, then *we'll* be the ones to starve. Pile lots of rocks over those fish if you don't want to go hungry later on."

So they built massive rock cairns over the buried fish, and over the supplies of dry caribou meat as well. On top of each cairn Awasin placed a caribou skull with the antlers pointing skyward. "That's our marker," he explained. "When the snows get deep we'd never find the caches without something sticking up to guide us."

Fish and meat were not the only foods the boys gathered. Out on the plains the dwarf scrub had turned to flaming orange under the touch of the frosts, and in the muskegs there were carpets of low plants whose leaves were turning a brilliant yellow. These did not look as if they could be much use, but Awasin carefully gathered from these plants a pile of leaves that had not yet been frostbitten. He dried the leaves in the frying pan, and packed away about fifteen pounds in a deerskin bag. The

123

Indians of the north have many names for this herb, but white men call it Labrador tea. When it is steeped in boiling water it makes a fair substitute for tea, and it was to be the only drink — except cold water — that the boys would have that winter.

The scanty arctic plants provided another and even more welcome addition to the food supplies. Crowberries and bearberries were to be found in the low muskegs, almost hidden in the moss. The boys spent two full days searching them out, and finally collected almost fifty pounds of the wizened little berries, which were already partly dried. The drying process was completed over the fire so the berries would not ferment later on. Then Awasin took half of them and mixed them with ground-up dry deermeat (that they had pulverized between two stones) and with boiling-hot deer fat. This rather sickening-looking mixture was then poured out to cool in slabs, and the slabs carefully wrapped in deerskin and put away. This was pemmican, and as Awasin said, it would be vitally important trail food when they began the long winter trek southward to the forests.

When they were searching for berries they met many competitors. The frosts had brought a wave of ptarmigan down from the north, and these arctic partridges were already turning white in preparation for the winter. They fed on the berries in such huge flocks that they looked like blankets of new snow upon the ground. They looked fat and tasty, and the two boys eyed them hungrily. But they did not dare waste precious ammunition on such small

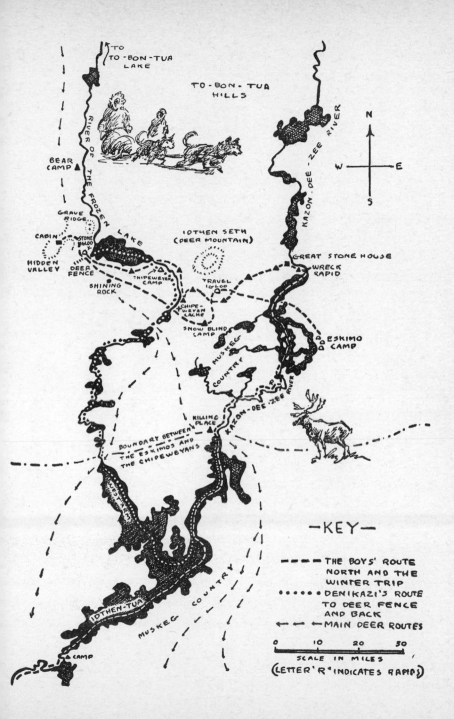

TO
TO-BON-TUA
LAKE

TO-BON-TUA
HILLS

RIVER OF THE FROZEN LAKE

KAZON-DEE-ZEE RIVER

N
W E
S

BEAR
CAMP

GRAVE
RIDGE

CABIN
STONE
IGLOO

HIDDEN
VALLEY

DEER
FENCE

SHINING
ROCK

IDTHEN SETH
(DEER MOUNTAIN)

CHIPEWEYAN
CAMP

TRAVEL
IGLOO

CHIPE-
WEYAN
CACHE

SNOW BLIND
CAMP

GREAT STONE HOUSE

WRECK
RAPID

MUSKEG
COUNTRY

ESKIMO
CAMP

KILLING
PLACE

KAZON-DEE-ZEE RIVER

BOUNDARY BETWEEN
THE ESKIMOS AND
THE CHIPEWEYANS

IDTHEN-TUA

MUSKEG COUNTRY

CAMP

-KEY-

- - - - THE BOYS' ROUTE
NORTH AND THE
WINTER TRIP
• • • • • DENIKAZI'S ROUTE
TO DEER FENCE
AND BACK
← ← ← MAIN DEER ROUTES

0   10   20   30
SCALE IN MILES
(LETTER "R" INDICATES RAPIDS)

game, so there were no chicken dinners. Awasin would not use a shell even on the many Canada geese that lingered on the tundra ponds.

The herds of doe caribou had dwindled away until hardly any deer were to be seen at the deer fence. This worried Jamie considerably, though Awasin stoutly insisted that the bucks would soon be along.

Once or twice Jamie eyed the pet fawn speculatively, for if it was a case of eat or die, the fawn was, after all, a caribou. The fawn seemed to understand these glances and to outdo itself in being friendly. It romped about the camp like a dog and followed them everywhere. Sometimes it was a nuisance, for it would bury its muzzle in the skin bags of berries and in a few seconds gulp down the work of hours. But taken all round, the boys had become so attached to the little beast that they could forgive it almost any trick. It helped to make the world a less lonely place — and in the broad plains, loneliness was something to fear.

On the day of the first real snow the fawn crawled out of the igloo first, and when the boys appeared the little beast was snorting at the queer white stuff that lay all about. It tasted the snow and spat it out hurriedly, leaping high into the air with disgust. The boys stood by laughing until the significance of the snowfall struck Jamie.

"Listen, Awasin," he said abruptly. "We've *got* to do something about fuel! All the food in the world won't help us if we're going to freeze to death."

Now at last the problem was out in the open. They ate a

gloomy breakfast. When the meal was over, Awasin was restless, anxious to do something about the wood supply.

"Let's make a trip up into the hills to the west," he said. "Maybe we can find something that will burn."

Willingly Jamie agreed, and after packing food, ammunition and the rifle they set off, closely followed by the fawn.

The sun came bleakly over the hills and its weakened rays began to melt the snow — but the threat of winter still remained.

The hills rose some five hundred feet above the valley floor, and though their lower slopes were carpeted with moss and lichens, their upper slopes and crests were bare. Built by the glaciers, the hills were really no more than gigantic rock piles. They looked harsh and forbidding.

Halfway up the mile-long slope Jamie's interest was aroused by a broad band of gravel running along below the crest of the hills. "That's a queer-looking thing," he said. "I wonder what it is and how it got there?"

When they reached the gravel streak the boys examined it curiously. It was about twenty feet wide and perfectly level. It ran south and north along the face of the hills as far as the eye could see. Above and below it were huge, angular chunks of rock, but the strip itself was composed of small rounded stones.

"It looks like a beach along a lake shore," Jamie said. "The rocks are rounded just as if they had been rubbed against each other by the waves." He dropped to his knees and began to dig among the stones. Then he scrambled to

128

his feet holding a tiny object in his hand. "It must have been a lake shore," he said. "Look at this, Awasin."

In his hand he held a tiny sea shell, so old that when Awasin took it, it crumbled into dust between his fingers.

Jamie looked out over the broad valley to the dim blue line of the hills to the east. He spoke with awe. "Thousands, maybe a million years ago, this must have been one huge ocean," he said. "And these hills were just little islands in it."

Awasin was not as surprised as Jamie expected him to be. "There's a Cree legend about that," he replied. "It tells of a time when the whole northern plains were all water and the water was filled with strange monsters."

Jamie nodded. "This seems to prove that story," he said. "But if the water was up this high then it must have covered everything as far as Reindeer Lake. I guess when it dried up it left Reindeer Lake as one of its little puddles."

Awasin laughed at the idea of mighty Reindeer being a puddle. "Well, let's get on," he said. "We can't burn these pebbles."

Now they were forced to jump from one sharp-edged boulder to the next. The whole face of the hill was a tortured chaos of fragmented stone, split to knife edges by the winter frosts.

Near the crest they stopped in awe at what they saw ahead. Stretching to the horizon was a series of mounded hills rising steadily upward. These hills were like the one they stood upon — great piles of shattered rock. The wind howled over the grim slopes, and racing gray clouds hung

129

low above the dismal peaks. Not a living thing broke the dreary monotony of the scene — not even a soaring raven.

"It looks like the end of the world," Jamie said. "Or maybe like the moon. Let's have a quick look at the other side."

Rather unwillingly Awasin followed Jamie.

What they saw at the crest left them speechless. Far below ran a narrow valley whose walls were slopes of broken boulders like the hills, but the valley floor was a paradise. A dozen tiny lakes lay along it in a chain and they shone like green mirrors. Around them were green swales and, most unbelievable of all, by the lake shores were stands of trees! They were *real* trees. White spruces and tamaracks towered fifty feet in the still air. It was a sight so unexpected that they could hardly believe it.

"If those *are* trees, then they will burn!" Awasin said in a hushed voice.

They were trees — no doubt of that. Jamie and Awasin had stumbled on one of the most amazing secrets of the arctic plains. Here and there, hidden deep in almost impenetrable ranges of rock hills, are a few protected valleys where the bitter blast of the arctic winds cannot reach. In these valleys trees gain a foothold, grasses and flowers follow as their seeds are carried by the birds, and so hidden sanctuaries from the bleakness of the Barrens are formed.

The boys stared in wonder at the sight below, but the little fawn was not so awed. With a pleased grunt it jumped over the edge and began slithering down the long and broken slope.

130

The spell was broken. "Hey!" Jamie yelled. "Come back here, you!" But the fawn kept happily on its way. Recklessly they followed, leaping from rock to rock like a pair of mountain goats. At last they reached the floor of the valley, and the trees loomed above them.

CHAPTER 16

The Coming of the Bucks

TOGETHER THEY HURRIED TO THE shore of the nearest lake and looked down into the clear green water. They could see the lazy forms of trout ten feet below the surface. A flock of late ducks rose and wheeled overhead. Out on the lake a pair of loons cried their idiot laughter.

Then they walked to the nearest stand of trees. Jamie looked up to the swaying tops of the spruces with a speculative eye. "A good spot to build a cabin," he said.

Before Awasin could answer there was a diversion. The little fawn suddenly went tearing off through the trees. Awasin caught a glimpse of distant movement and unslung the rifle. Then he and Jamie ran to the edge of the woods for a better view.

They were in time to see a herd of about fifty buck caribou come leisurely out from among the trees and begin grazing on a patch of sedge.

Awasin's face was alive with excitement. "Those bucks must have been here all summer long," he said. "And I'll bet they stay all winter too! If they do, we can have fresh meat whenever we need it!"

Quietly they retreated so as not to disturb the herd. Jamie noticed that the fawn was still missing. "I guess we've lost our pet," he said.

"Never mind him now," Awasin replied. "Let's explore the rest of this valley."

For the next two hours they examined the new world they had found. The valley was not large — perhaps four miles long, and not more than half a mile wide at any point. Each little lake had its own stand of tamaracks, and spruces huddled under the northern wall of the valley.

Because it offered easy walking, the boys climbed a queer sand ridge that ran down the center of the valley. It was about forty feet high and three feet wide at the top. The sides were so steep that the boys were winded when they reached the crest. A well-marked game trail, packed down by the feet of wolves and deer, was hollowed into the narrow top of the sand ridge. The ridge itself ran the full length of the valley and it was so regular in shape that Jamie, in astonishment, suggested that it looked like an old highway embankment. "Looks more like a riverbed upside down," Awasin said. And he was closer to the truth.

The sand ridge was an esker — and eskers are among the most curious formations on earth. They were produced by the great glaciers that once covered the Barrens plains to a depth of several thousand feet with solid ice.

When at last the glaciers began to melt, they formed rivers on their surfaces. Gradually these rivers cut down through the ice until they were running through vast tunnels. Often they cut through pockets of gravel and sand that had been scooped up by the moving ice sheet, and before long the rivers were building beds for themselves in the center of the icecap.

After many more thousands of years the glaciers disappeared, and their rivers vanished with them. But the glacier riverbeds remained. They were dropped down by the melting ice onto the solid land beneath — the beds of rivers, turned upside down, just as Awasin had suggested.

Now they run across hills, valleys, plains and lakes without regard for the present shapes and slopes of the land. Some are hundreds of miles long and they may even cross mountain ranges in the same way that the Great Wall of China snakes its way up and down mountains. In places the eskers drive straight across big lakes like causeways. They are the natural highways of the arctic plains.

Awasin and Jamie used their esker as a road, for from

134

its smooth and level crest they could look down on the valley as they walked easily along. They followed it to the west end of the valley where the sand ridge climbed up the steep rock slopes into the hills. They turned back then, and by late afternoon had reached the valley's eastern end. Here the esker descended through a steep cleft downward out of the green valley. The boys followed, and after two miles suddenly emerged through a gully into the broad and barren valley of the River of the Frozen Lake! Below them, and a few miles south, they could faintly see the line of the deer fence and they could even pick out the tiny dot that was their stone igloo.

It was the final stroke of luck in a very lucky day. If they had been forced to carry supplies up over the rocky hills, and down again into the hidden valley, it would have been a backbreaking job. But now they had a ready-made highway over which they could come and go with ease.

The sun was setting as they stood looking down into the plains. "My people would say that Manitou was with us," Awasin said quietly. It was a solemn moment — but it did not stay solemn for long.

A tired grunt from behind made the boys turn around. There, making its way wearily down the esker, was the missing fawn. Its sleek coat was rumpled and it looked as if it had spent the afternoon in a football scrimmage. Meekly it came up to them, nuzzled Jamie's hand, and flopped down at their feet.

"I should have thought of that," Awasin chuckled.

135

"Thought of what?" Jamie asked.

"Why, of those bucks," Awasin replied. "With the mating season coming on, the old fellows get mean. They won't let a young deer come near them. They probably chased this fellow of ours right down the valley!"

"Well, there's only bucks left in the country now so I guess we'll have this youngster with us all winter," Jamie said. "We ought to give him a name. I'm getting tired of calling him Hey You."

"How about Otanak!" Awasin suggested. "It means the backward one — the one who got left behind."

"Good enough," said Jamie. "Come on, Otanak, no supper for anyone till we get home."

That night they made plans. They would make their main camp in the hidden valley. There they could build a comfortable cabin and have an unlimited supply of firewood. But still many serious problems remained.

There was the question of food. Finding the herd of bucks in Hidden Valley was a help — if the bucks stayed all winter. But the boys urgently needed prime hides for their winter clothing. Also, and even more important, they had to have a much greater stock of fat to see them through the winter. This meant remaining at Stone Igloo Camp, as the boys now called it, until the bucks had come.

Jamie had been keeping track of the days by cutting little nicks in the edge of the lead sheet from the Viking tomb. Now he did some calculating. "I think it's about September fifteenth," he said, "and that means we'll be

136

lucky if the winter doesn't hit us in a week. Maybe the bucks have already gone south some other way."

"I doubt it," Awasin replied. "The bucks don't move until the first heavy snow. Then they go fast. We must act quickly when they come."

The next morning saw two inches of new snow on the ground. After breakfast Awasin climbed inland to get a view up the valley to the north.

For a long time he could see nothing moving over the white stretch of the valley. Then his quick eyes caught a tiny movement in the pale northern skies. He watched till he was sure. "Ravens!" he whispered at last. "The Black Ones — the brothers of the deer are moving."

He strained his eyes until they hurt, and at last he was rewarded. Many miles to the north he saw something that looked like the flicker of heat waves on an August day. There was no doubt about it now. Far up the river valley the white snows had disappeared and it was as if the whole landscape was moving. A great wave of deer was flowing down the valley with the slow but resistless motion of a wall of lava flowing from a volcano.

Awasin raced back to camp. "An hour — maybe two — and they'll be here!" he cried breathlessly. "Hurry!"

They put out the fire and scattered the glowing lumps of moss. Everything loose went into the stone igloo. Then they made their way to the gap in the deer fence.

During the preceding days Awasin had visited the stone pillars in the fence and had put a lump of loose sphagnum moss on top of each. Now as the morning

137

breeze played down the valley it stirred the moss and made it seem that each of the pillars was a living thing — a hunter waiting for his prey.

No deer were in sight, but already there was a faint familiar odor — the barnyard stench upon the breeze. Quickly they completed their plans. Jamie was to take the rifle this time, and hide in one of the hunting pits near the gap. With Awasin's assistance he heaped up a pile of boulders in front of the pit to act as a barrier to the deer.

Awasin had equipped himself with a homemade spear made from a short piece of spruce brought home from Hidden Valley and tipped with his hunting knife. He took up a position on the opposite side of the gap behind a huge square chunk of rock.

They waited, and as the suspense grew, Jamie remembered what old Denikazi had said about the migration of the bucks: "They come like thunder, and for the space of a day the world is theirs. Then like the thunder they are gone, and nothing moves upon the frozen plains till spring returns again." Jamie knew that every shot would have to count. He crouched low, watching with straining eyes a ridge a half mile to the north that cut off the view up the valley.

Suddenly the crest of the ridge underwent an amazing change. It was as though a forest had sprouted on that naked hill. Thousands upon thousands of twisting branches seemed to be springing from the rocky ground and waving gently in the breeze.

Jamie knew the trees were the antlers of the deer

138

coming up the far slope. He pressed the butt of the rifle tightly against his shoulder.

Now the deer had reached the crest and were breasting it. Their antlers thrust high into the air, and the beasts were moving in such a compact mass that their broad horns formed one impenetrable hedge of bone.

They swept over the ridge and down towards the fence while another mass of beasts replaced them on the crest. In mere moments it seemed to Jamie that the entire world was hidden under the brown bodies of the deer.

The smell was so strong that he began to choke. His ears were deafened by the clicking of ankle joints, and of antlers striking antlers. A kind of panic overwhelmed him and he fired wildly into the throng.

Certain that he must be crushed into pulp beneath those myriad feet, he ran up a small rocky hillock that stood out like an island to breast the approaching flood. From the precarious top of this mound Jamie began firing again.

His shots had no perceptible effect. Six or seven animals reared up momentarily, then disappeared beneath the press of bodies. The caribou were too tightly compressed, and too imbued by the urge of the moment, to pay any attention to the puny efforts of a boy and a gun. They did not swerve, nor slow. Irresistible as the sea itself they flowed steadily forward.

Awasin, on his side of the gap, was almost as overcome as Jamie had been. He too was afraid of being trampled to death, but his hunting training came to his rescue. Yelling like a fiend, he leaped to his feet and began thrusting with his homemade spear at the beasts that hemmed him in. Soon a mound of bodies grew up about him like the breastwork of a fortress. The deer continued past, swirling about the islet where the Indian boy stood, soaked in blood, and wild with the excitement of the moment.

Jamie, on his pinnacle of rock, had begun to realize that there was no real danger. The bucks made no attempt to harm him. He believed he could have descended from his rock and stood in the middle of the multitude and been unharmed, for the deer would have flowed around him, leaving him untouched. Just the same he stayed where he was, but his panic was gone. Now he fired only an occasional shot when a particularly fat buck came close by. After half an hour he stopped. Enough deer were dead.

The endless movement of the deer began to hypnotize him. He sat still as a statue while the tremendous impact of the spectacle gradually registered on his mind. The heaving, seething sea of antlers and brown backs flowed on. Time passed like light. The flood poured on . . .

It must have been several hours later that Jamie looked down from his perch and saw no living deer. Instead he saw the bloody figure of Awasin walking toward him. Stiffly Jamie lowered himself from the rocks.

The world was very still and motionless.

They met beneath the rock pile and said not a word to each other. Silently they walked back to their camp, each alone with his own thoughts. Never, while they lived, would they forget this day — for they had looked deeply into one of the great mysteries of the animal world.

140

CHAPTER 17

Building a Home

NEITHER HAD MUCH APPETITE FOR dinner. The reaction from the slaughter was so great that they did not even talk of preparing the meat they had killed. They had seen too much blood that day, and too much death.

The sound of foxes barking finally aroused them.

"They're up by the gap," Jamie said after listening for a

while, "eating the deer, I guess. Maybe we should go back and fix things up."

Awasin slowly nodded his head. "That's right," he replied at last. "We have to finish the job. If we let those deer go to waste now we'll be no better than murderers."

It was a long job and an unpleasant one. For the next four days they were constantly busy either at the carcasses of the forty-seven bucks they had killed, or at Stone Igloo Camp, where they were preparing the meat and the prime hides. There was still enough heat in the pale sun to dry partly the fine hides taken from the bucks, and the frosts at night were heavy enough so that no special care was needed with the meat. It was merely packed away under rock piles near the camp.

The biggest task was the preparation of the fat. They kept the fire going all day, and for most of each night. The tea-billy hung over the fire all the time, filled with fat.

There were two kinds of fat, and they had to be prepared separately. The suet could simply be cut into chunks and boiled until it became liquid. Every now and again Jamie would pour off the hot grease into the frying pan, which he had fixed in the moss on a piece of ice. When the pan cooled he had another five-pound slab of suet to add to the steadily growing pile.

The most valuable fat was what could be boiled out of the bone marrow. They had collected all the leg bones and, using the hatchet, Awasin smashed these to pulp. Jamie then boiled them and skimmed off the rich yellow stuff that

142

floated to the surface. It was slow work because the tea pail was so small, but at the end of the fourth day they had ten blocks of marrowfat that was soft and creamy and tasted rather like butter. In addition they had thirty blocks of hard, waxy lard melted down from the body fat.

During this period they continued to lift the net each day. Since the weather was now cold enough to preserve the fish, they did not bother trying to dry them, but simply cleaned them and rocked them down. But on a morning near the end of September there was an inch of ice over the little bay in the river and the net came out for the last time. The big lake too was frozen over, and the only open water was at the rapids.

Now it was time to move into Hidden Valley. One cold, bright day, accompanied by Otanak, they set off, carrying some camp equipment, their tools, and a week's supply of food. All the rest of their stores lay under rock caches, or were carefully stowed away in the stone igloo. Later, when the snows were deep, they planned to build a sled to carry the remainder of their supplies to Hidden Valley.

Before leaving, Jamie took a careful inventory of the stock of food. It made a most impressive total.

Over a hundred whitefish and trout had been partly dried or smoked, and nearly as many fresh trout were frozen under the moss. Packed away in the stone igloo were two hundred pounds of lard and marrowfat; sixty pounds of dried deermeat; some pemmican; forty pounds of dry

143

berries; fifteen pounds of Labrador tea; and a good pile of deer tongues. The deerskins and the hanks of sinew were also stored away in the igloo.

Scattered about near the camp were half a dozen stone caches containing the balance of the deermeat. It was a good big larder — more than sufficient, and as long as it was available the boys would never starve.

In Hidden Valley they at once set about picking a site for their cabin. The valley was divided into three parts, like beads strung along the esker ridge. Each of these parts had its section of forest and one or more small lakes. The center section soon proved itself the best. Behind a ten-acre stand of trees an abrupt cliff shielded the spot from the north. And right in the center of the woods was a little lake, big enough to supply drinking water and so well protected that there was a chance it might not freeze clear to the bottom even in midwinter. The esker, that natural highway, ran right past the small lake and anyone living in this spot could travel to either end of the valley in less than an hour.

At dusk they pitched a temporary camp in the woods, and that night they lay by a roaring spruce fire, making plans.

With the dawn they were up and anxious to get to work. They chose a small clearing in the center of the woods, near the lake, where the ground was fairly level. Then they separated into the forest to seek out, and blaze, enough trees for the cabin walls.

It was then they began to realize that the job was not

going to be so easy after all. There was lots of timber, but it was of an unusual kind. The trees were thick at the base but the trunks tapered very sharply — like inverted ice-cream cones — towards the tops. Slow growth, and the struggle with the elements, had made them this way. There were practically no straight logs the proper length for cabin walls. Also, the little hatchet had never been meant for chopping down trees a foot in diameter. It took them a full hour of backbreaking labor to chew down their first tree. Then it took another hour to chop off the gnarled and stone-hard branches. By dusk, which fell in early after-noon, they had one tree down — but the log they cut from it was too heavy to be dragged back to the cabin site.

Dispirited and miserable, they sat about the fire that evening. They had hoped to have their cabin built in a week or ten days, but now they realized that it might be springtime before they were ready to move in. They were a gloomy pair as they stretched their sore muscles and shiv-ered in the night frost.

After a long, glum silence, Jamie spoke. "Well," he said, "we must make up our minds that we can't do it. At least not the way we planned."

Morosely, Awasin agreed. The original plan had been to build a cabin twelve feet square, laying the logs up in rows and notching them at the corners. This would have re-quired fourteen-foot logs in order to allow for the overlap at the ends. Now the boys had found they could hardly manage to chop down a tree that would make a fourteen-foot log, and if they managed that much, the log was not

145

only too heavy to haul back to camp, but its ends differed so much in size that it was almost useless anyway.

Jamie sat looking into the fire. Occasionally he glanced up at the black walls of the forest in front of him. "Look at all that wood," he said, "standing up there as thick as hairs on a dog's back." Then slowly an idea began to take form in his mind. "If those trees were only a few inches apart, instead of five or six feet apart," he thought, "they'd form a solid *upright* wall!" He considered the idea for a moment longer.

Then he jumped up and shouted. "That's *it!* We'll set the logs on *end*, then we won't need them more than six or seven feet long!"

Thinking it out as he went along, Jamie explained his idea in detail. Awasin grew enthusiastic and began adding ideas of his own. They talked for an hour, and when they finally crawled under the deerskins for the night they were in a cheerful and happy mood. The new plan looked like the answer.

Now they wanted logs ranging from five to eight feet long, and these could be cut from much smaller trees. After three days of constant hacking and chopping they had a pile of twenty or thirty logs beside their chosen site. Then they began construction.

The work was largely a matter of trial and error, and there were some fierce arguments about the ways and means. Jamie wanted to use two living trees, that were about the right distance apart, for the back corner posts. Awasin wanted the cabin centered in the clearing, and he

146

won out. The first chore was to dig four holes (using the frying pan as a shovel), as deep as possible, at the four corners. This was not difficult, since the clearing was on a thick bed of sand washed down from the esker and there was no permanent ground frost in it. When the holes were down three feet and touching solid rock, they carefully erected the corner posts. The two in front were seven feet above the ground level, while the two back posts stuck up only five feet.

The next job was to tie pairs of saplings crosswise between each pair of corner poles — one sapling inside and one outside in each pair. There were two pairs for each wall, a lower pair a foot above the ground and an upper pair a foot from the tops of the corner posts.

Jamie had been about to use the precious rope for the tying job until Awasin stopped him. "*Babiche* will do that job better," Awasin said, and he set about making some Indian rope.

First of all he took a deer hide and scraped and cut all the hair from it. Next he soaked it till it was soft, pegged it out on the ground, and made a slit in the edge near one corner. From here he began a spiral knife-cut that went round and round, cutting off a strip about an inch in width. By the time Awasin had reached the center of the hide, he had a piece of skin an inch wide and almost a hundred feet in length.

He soaked this for an hour in warm water, then took it in his hands and rolled it between his palms, starting at one end and working along to the other. Back and forth he went, and as the hide slowly dried it began to form a round, rawhide rope a quarter inch thick and as strong as the best hemp line.

When a piece was needed, they soaked it until it was soft, then tied the logs in place. As the rawhide dried it shrank, and the joint became as tight as if it had been spiked.

The work went very slowly. After two days of building the boys had only the framework completed. It measured ten feet square, seven feet high in front and five feet at the back.

The next chore was cutting the wall logs. These had to be a little smaller than the corner logs, so that they could be slipped between the horizontal pairs of saplings. The back wall was fairly easy, for all the logs in it were the same length, but the sides were another matter, since they sloped from front to back, and each new log had to be a different length from its neighbor.

It took three days to build each side wall, and two days each for the back and front walls.

The door was easy. They simply left out four of the upright logs in the center of the front wall. For a window there was a narrow opening, one log deep, covered with a thinly scraped piece of deerskin to let in a little light.

Ten days after beginning construction, the walls were up. And it was none too soon. On the tenth day the boys had to make a trip to Stone Igloo Camp for more food, and when they emerged from Hidden Valley they were startled by the change in the world below them. The plains had vanished beneath a heavy fall of snow. The lakes and rivers had disappeared as well, and only slight depressions in the white blanket showed where they had been.

There had, of course, been snow in Hidden Valley while the boys were working. But the sun, striking on the protected slopes, had generated enough heat to melt it soon after it fell. Out on the plains the snow lay deep, and winter had come at last.

It was a bitterly cold and frightening trip to Stone Igloo Camp and back into Hidden Valley. They sighed with relief when they were again on the esker and walking on snow-free sand.

"It's a good thing we found this valley," Jamie said. "I'd hate to spend the winter out there on the frozen plains."

"We had good luck," Awasin replied, "but we'd better not stretch it. Winter will hit this valley soon. We must hurry and finish the cabin."

With renewed energy they tackled the roof. They worked hard to keep warm. Even in the protected valley they were beginning to suffer from the cold. Their blanket-coats were awkward and not very effective.

After several searches through the valley they managed to find a dozen slender poles some twelve feet in length. These they used as rafters, letting them overhang the walls a foot on each side to protect the rawhide lashings on the logs from the weather. They planned to make a flat, or "shanty," roof, sloping from front to back, but before they began laying the covering on the rafters they took time out for a hot meal and a good warming by the fire.

Awasin was just putting some deer tongue slices on to fry when a thought struck him. He dropped the pan and whirled around to where Jamie was sipping a mug of Labrador tea.

"Jamie!" he cried. "What are we going to do for a stove, or a stovepipe!"

Jamie's mouth fell open. "It never crossed my mind!" he admitted foolishly. "Guess I just took it for granted that when we were ready for a stove, we'd have one handy. D'you think we could build a fireplace of stones and chink it up with mud?"

Awasin retrieved the deer tongues and started them cooking. "No," he replied shortly. "It would fall apart as soon as the heat got to it. The only thing I can think of is an open fireplace in the middle of the cabin, and let the smoke rise up through the roof."

Jamie looked dubious. "There'd be room for the smoke — but not for us too," he said. "Even with a big smoke hole, that flat roof will hold the smoke down and most of it'll stay inside. We'd choke to death in no time."

For a moment Awasin didn't answer. Then he said, "Our roof slopes up toward the front. Suppose we made it a peak roof, then it would slope up to the middle as well. It would make a sort of channel to take the smoke to the highest point at the front, where we'd leave a smoke hole for it to get out."

Jamie looked impressed as Awasin continued: "There's another thing. We should leave holes under the walls to let fresh air in. When I was young my family lived all one

150

winter in a tent and my mother always kept one edge of the tent raised so a draft could carry off the smoke."

"A darn cold draft, I'll bet," Jamie replied. "Why couldn't we dig a tunnel from outside, with the inside end opening right beside the fire? That way there'd be no hurricane blowing across the floor."

All through the meal they discussed the problem. Awasin's experience and Jamie's inventiveness at last combined to give them what looked like a good answer. That afternoon they untied the roof rafters, added a ridgepole, and rebuilt the framework of the roof, filling in the gable ends with short pieces of logs.

The next morning they gathered armfuls of willows and lashed these in place across the rafters. Then they added a foot-thick layer of sphagnum moss. On top of everything they tied caribou hides, overlapping them like huge shingles. To hold the hides down they laid on more poles, and weighted these with rocks. At the front end of their roof they left a hole the size of a water pail to serve as the chimney.

Since the cabin was almost finished, they now moved in. But the many chinks in the walls still had to be filled with moss, a door had to be made, and the fireplace built. While Awasin did the other jobs, Jamie worked on the fireplace.

First he built a circle of stones about three feet across and a foot high, in the middle of the floor. He filled this with sand, then on top placed a half-circle of flat rocks set on edge. After a long search on the hill slopes, he found two thin stones about two feet long and six inches wide. These he placed across his half-circle to provide a rest for the frying pan, or to be used as a sort of stove-top for general cooking. Finally he took the hatchet and scratched out a tunnel across the floor, under the logs, and a few feet beyond the cabin wall. This he roofed with stones and covered with sand, leaving both ends open.

At last he was done. He gathered a pile of firewood and called out to Awasin, "Ready to give her a try!"

Awasin hurried inside and they both watched tensely as a piece of burning wood from the outside campfire caught the kindling. The smoke began to rise. But instead of heading up and out the chimney hole, it settled happily back into the room about their shoulders. Soon they were coughing, their eyes streaming tears. They stood it as long as they could, but finally had to stumble out into the fresh air.

Still coughing, Awasin said, "Give it time, Jamie, it may work better when the room heats up."

Jamie was depressed. He looked up at the roof, where the merest trickle of smoke was coming through the hole, turned away and began walking toward the old campsite.

A shout from Awasin stopped him. "Jamie! Look quick!"

Slowly Jamie turned his head, then he spun about and stared. The smoke was pouring out the chimney hole in a thick rolling cloud that rose above the trees and drifted off down the valley.

Awasin had pushed aside the deerskin that was doing temporary service as a door. "Come inside!" he called.

Jamie came running, and there was no smoke pall to

152

greet him. Instead there was a cheerful blaze in the fireplace, and the room was already comfortably warm. The smoke rose straight up to the roof, rolled along under the peak, and vanished out the hole. Fresh air from the tunnel poured in at the fireplace and was heated by the flames.

"I guess I was too darn impatient," Jamie said as he squatted by the fire. "This outfit works better than most camp stoves."

Awasin grinned. "Let's put on a brew of tea to celebrate."

As Awasin had guessed, the reason for the smoke trouble had been that warm air rises, while cold air normally sinks. When the fire was first lit there was a good deal of smoke but little heat, and so there was no rising draft of warm air to carry the smoke up and out the chimney. Once the room began to heat up, the air rose steadily, lifting the smoke with it.

That night they slept comfortably on beds of moss in their new home. When they dozed off they were as proud as if they had built a castle.

They had reason to be proud. Good sense and hard work had conquered the last of their major problems. Now, barring some unforeseen misfortune, they were almost certain to survive the winter in the dreaded Barrenlands.

During the first week after moving into the cabin there was a lot of carpentry work to finish. Bunks had to be built of saplings set against the north wall, then covered with mattresses of sphagnum moss and caribou hides. Sleeping robes had to be made as well, and these consisted of deer hides placed with the fur side in, and sewed along three edges.

Jamie built a table of flat rocks raised on stones to about two feet above the floor. Since there were no chairs, this was high enough. The boys crouched on two boulders, each of which had a cushion of caribou hide, and dined in style.

Three saplings lashed to a framework against the side walls served as shelves. The old canoe rope crisscrossed the ceiling as a clothesline from which wet moccasins and garments could be hung to dry.

The camp routine was simple. Each was to be cook for a week at a time. The cook — Awasin had the first shift — got up first each morning to renew the fire and start breakfast. This usually consisted of Labrador tea, fried trout (that had been thawed out the night before), and perhaps some stew left over from supper. In the meantime Jamie went to the little lake for water. After chopping through the new ice he would fill a skin bag, made from scraped deer hide, and let it soak for a while until the sinew thread swelled and made the joints watertight. As long as there was water in the bag it remained waterproof, but as soon as it dried out, broad cracks appeared along the seams.

After breakfast there was the wood supply to see to. They suspected that by midwinter heavy drifts would have piled into the valley and it might be difficult to get wood, and harder still to drag it home. So they spent as much time as possible searching out dead trees, cutting them up, and dragging them to camp. Even though the weather was not yet bitterly cold, it took a lot of wood to keep the

154

cabin warm — particularly at night, when the fire was kept alive with chunks of green spruce that burned slowly.

Twice in the first week at the cabin they made trips to Stone Igloo Camp for supplies, and each time they felt the cold more intensely and were increasingly aware that something would have to be done about clothing.

The day that Jamie took over as cook was, according to the notches cut in the lead plate, November 1. He had the fire roaring before Awasin crawled out of his sleeping bag, but the cabin was still uncomfortably cold.

Awasin shivered as he dressed. Then he stepped outside to go for water. Jamie could hear his moccasins crunching in the snow, testifying to how cold it was. Half an hour later he was back, looking half frozen. "It's really winter out!" he said through chattering teeth. "We must have some winter clothes or we soon won't be able to go out at all."

Breakfast over, they turned their full attention to the problem. Several prime hides were stored in the cabin, and Awasin had already cleaned these thoroughly on the inside and partially smoke-tanned them.

Jamie suggested that he use his old and tattered trousers for a pattern. He took them off and carefully cut the threads along the seams. Then he laid the worn pieces of cloth on a caribou hide, and with his pocketknife cut the hide to the same shape.

The idea worked well enough for trousers, but jackets were a different matter. "Maybe we should make pullover parkas like the Eskimos'," was Jamie's suggestion.

155

"That's the best idea," Awasin replied. "But we'll have to make them with hoods. Too bad we don't have wolf fur to trim them with."

"Why is wolf fur so special?" Jamie wanted to know.

"Because it and wolverine fur are the only kinds your breath won't form ice on," Awasin answered patiently. "Any other kind of fur ices up and may stick to you and freeze your face."

"I'll shoot the next one I see, then," Jamie promised as he went back to the problem of laying out a pattern for a parka.

While Jamie cut and fitted, Awasin sewed. They worked steadily all day and by nightfall had one complete pair of trousers to show for the effort, plus a big pile of scraps of hide and spoiled or discarded pieces.

The fur on the trousers was turned in and the hair was against the wearer's bare skin. Tying the moccasin tops around the ankles of the trousers made a good tight join. Though they looked bulky and awkward, the trousers were warm and comfortable. But they had to be kept dry. Once wet, they hardened and became like sheet metal.

During the next day Jamie worked doggedly to cut out a parka. Half a dozen times he cut the pieces the way he thought they should be, and then "tacked" them together with a few stitches, only to find that the garment was hopelessly ill-fitting.

The cold outside was worse that day, and Jamie knew he could not give in. Cut — sew — rip apart — and try

156

again. It was growing dusk before he had a model that looked as if it might possibly do.

He left it till next morning. But Awasin had been more successful that day and now there were three pairs of fur trousers hanging on the clothesline near the ceiling. Awasin's job had not been easy. Sewing with the limber bone needles took hours of slow labor. Both the seams and the sinew had to be kept moist all the time, and the needle holes had to be made in advance with the fishhook.

In two more days the parkas were finished. They hung to the knees and looked like outsize turtle-neck sweaters. Attached to the back of each was a hood that could be pulled well forward over the face. The boys dressed themselves in their new outfits with their old cotton shirts on underneath. Then they looked at each other and laughed.

"Well, never mind the looks," said Awasin. "I think these outfits will be warm. We'll try a trip sometime soon and see."

As it happened they needed to make a trip even sooner than Awasin guessed, for that night they had a most unwelcome visitor.

CHAPTER 18
Of Wolverines and Sleds

THE NEXT MORNING AWASIN WENT for water shortly after dawn, but he was back in a few moments without the water. Just outside he had found the tracks of a wolverine, and when he investigated he discovered that the robber had destroyed the twenty pounds of deermeat stored on top of the cabin roof.

It was obvious that, having once found the meat, the wolverine would remain as a permanent, though uninvited, guest for the rest of the winter. So they had to spend

158

that day making a tree-cache where their supplies would be safe.

They chose four small trees growing close together, and lashed crosspieces to them about ten feet from the ground. Then they made a platform of saplings on the crosspieces to carry the weight of the food which was to be stored there. Finally they trimmed the bark off the tree trunks for several feet above ground level, and tied a collar of pointed sticks, facing downward, around each of the four trunks about six feet from the ground. Awasin completed the job by building a little ladder which could be moved away from the tree-cache after being used.

The next night Jamie was awakened by suspicious sounds outside. He called Awasin, then slid into his clothes and grabbed the rifle. Awasin stood at the open door holding a flaming piece of spruce while Jamie rushed out to the cache. By the faint, flickering light, Jamie could see a large shadow scuttling away toward the bush and he tried a quick shot at it, but apparently without results. The wolverine had made a mess of the cache. Bundles of frozen fish and meat lay scattered in the snow, and some of these had been broken open.

Not until morning did the boys discover how the wily wolverine had managed to raid the cache. Unable to climb the main supporting trunks, the animal had shinnied up a thin tamarack about a dozen feet to one side of the platform. Claw marks on the tamarack bark showed that the beast had kept his weight towards the cache, and as he climbed, the slender little tree had bent over like a bow.

159

When it was bent far enough the wolverine had only to let go and drop to the platform.

Somewhat awed by such a demonstration of cleverness, the boys spent several hours clearing away all the trees in the immediate vicinity of the cache.

"The Chipeweyans say wolverines aren't animals at all, but devils," Awasin commented feelingly as they restored the damage.

"That's putting it mildly," Jamie replied. "If that thing had been an animal I'd have killed it last night. I'm sure the bullet hit it, but there wasn't any blood, and no dead wolverine."

"Maybe you *did* hit it, Jamie," his friend said. "But they're about the hardest animal in the world to kill. I've seen them run away with a thirty-thirty slug right through them!"

An unpleasant thought occurred to Jamie. "Say!" he said. "If we've got wolverines around here, what about the stuff down at Stone Igloo Camp?"

"We'd better go and see," Awasin replied. "If the wolverines *have* been there we may have to cart *all* the stuff back here."

"Not on our backs, I hope," said Jamie anxiously. "We'd better build some kind of sled."

They needed a sled badly in any case. It could be used to haul supplies from Stone Igloo Camp, and also for bringing in loads of firewood. After breakfast they put their heads together over this new problem.

In the forest country sleds are seldom used, since the

160

snow among the trees is usually soft and deep, and sled runners sink in too far. Toboggans are used instead, but making these requires special tools and woods. However, the snow on the plains is of a different sort, for it is packed almost stone-hard by the winds and is ideal for sled runners.

"I once saw a Chipeweyan sled for use on the edge of the Barrens," Awasin said. "I think I can remember how it was made. But it was a big thing, almost fifteen feet long, and it needed ten dogs to pull it."

"Well," Jamie replied, "we'd better make ours a lot smaller. How about six feet long? If it's still too big we can chop a foot off it."

"We'll need two squared timbers for runners then," said Awasin. "And half a dozen crosspieces about two inches square and two feet long. Let's get the ax and go see what we can find."

It took the rest of the morning to locate, and fell, two trees suitable for runners. These were cut into six-foot logs and dragged into the cabin together with a number of small spruce saplings for crosspieces.

Awasin trimmed the logs with the ax while Jamie squared the crosspieces with the big hunting knife. When the runners were finished they were about four inches high, two inches thick, and their front ends were curved up a little so they would slide easily over humps and crevices. Awasin laid them side by side on the floor, about eighteen inches apart. Then he placed the crosspieces on top of them, at intervals of a foot.

"It looks good," Jamie said. "But how do we fasten all the pieces together?"

"*Babiche*," Awasin answered. "But somehow we have to drill holes through the runners, and we haven't any drill."

All afternoon the boys struggled to find a way to make the holes, but they had no luck. They tried using the blades of the small pocketknives, but these made hardly any impression on the hard green wood. At last Jamie put his knife away. "See if you can dream up another idea," he said, "while I get supper."

The fire was roaring on the hearth as Jamie leaned down to pick up the old frying pan. It had been sitting close to the flames and the handle — made of a piece of wire — was hot. Still thinking about the sled, Jamie thoughtlessly grasped the handle. The next minute he was bounding around the cabin, howling with pain.

When he stopped his wild prancing, there was a curious look on his face. He stared down at the frying pan. "I've got it!" he yelled. "That old wire handle! Heat it red hot and we can burn the holes in the runners!"

Awasin looked at him with real admiration. "That might work," he said. "Let's try it."

The idea did work, but it took a long time to burn a pair of holes through each runner, at the point where each crosspiece came. It was well after midnight when, working by the light of the fire, the crosspieces were at last lashed firmly to the runners with thin strips of wet rawhide.

"Not bad," Jamie said. "That hide will be dry by morning, and then the joints will be firm. Let's go to bed. Tomorrow we'll try out our new clothes and the sled too."

Early the next day the boys carried the new sled outdoors into a crisp, cold morning. Awasin rigged two pulling straps to the front of it while Jamie packed some camp gear and the sleeping robes, for now that winter had come it was not safe to go any distance unless prepared to spend the night if a sudden storm blew up. At last they put the loops of the pulling straps around their shoulders and gave the sled a try. It pulled like a solid chunk of lead!

Jamie was disappointed but Awasin was unperturbed. "I forgot," he said. "The Chipeweyans pour water on the runners and let it freeze, then they get an ice surface that will skid easily. Wait a moment . . ."

He ran for the water bucket and in a few moments had squirted several mouthfuls of water on the runners, where it froze almost at once. Then Awasin carefully scraped the surface smooth with his knife. "Let's try her now," he said.

This time the sled moved so easily that once it was in motion the boys hardly felt any pull against their shoulders.

Happily they set off, their breath forming white clouds about their parka hoods as they trotted down the valley.

When they emerged from the hills into the open plains a fierce north wind met them, but they turned their backs to it and on the hard-packed snow of the plains the sled fairly flew along toward Stone Igloo Camp.

When they reached the deer fence they found that the stone pillars had completely disappeared beneath the drifts. The meat caches had also vanished except for

163

the deer antlers Awasin had thoughtfully placed on top of each cairn as markers.

The stone igloo was snowed under and they had to use the hatchet to chop away the hard snow that had packed around the doorway. Jamie crawled in and to his relief found that the stored food and hides were untouched. No wolverine had broken in.

But Awasin had gone to investigate some of the nearby caches of meat, and he returned to report that one of them was ruined. "Come and look," he said, "and you'll see why I made such a fuss about heaping all those rocks on top of the meat."

At the cache Jamie was amazed to find that boulders weighing fifty pounds had been pried loose and rolled aside. The wolverines had done a thorough job. What they had not eaten had been left for foxes and wolves to finish and there was nothing left except a few fragments of bone.

"It's lucky they only smashed one cache," replied Awasin. "But we'd better get the meat up to the cabin where we can keep an eye on it."

They decided to have a quick meal, then load the sled and set off for home. Hauling all the food and other supplies up to the cabin was going to be no easy job and neither boy looked forward to it. "It's going to take a week of darn hard work," Jamie said gloomily. Then wistfully he added, "Wish we had a team of dogs."

They had one thing to be grateful for, however. Despite the cold wind, and the lack of a dinner fire, they were warm. The new clothing was more of a success than they had dared expect, though the makeshift gloves that Awasin had hurriedly put together as an afterthought were so clumsy that they had to be taken off when there was finger work to do.

After a cold dinner of pemmican, Jamie walked off to check the rest of the caches while Awasin began to load the sled. The Indian boy was startled by a sudden yell from Jamie.

"Come over here — quick!" Jamie called from one of the most distant caches. "And bring the rifle!"

Awasin ran to join him and found Jamie standing beside the cache. It was in a hollow and the snow that had drifted in was still soft enough to show footmarks. In a half-circle about the antlers that marked the cache was a ring of queer depressions in the snow. As Awasin looked at them he felt his back hair begin to prickle.

The marks were more than a foot in diameter, perfectly round, and about three feet apart. They looked as if they had been made with the end of a small barrel.

"What on earth could have made those!" Jamie whispered, for he too felt a sudden chill of fear.

Awasin was slow to answer. "Only two things I know of," he said, and his voice sounded thin and frightened, "and I don't want to meet *either* of them! They *might* be tracks of the giant Barrens grizzly bear — or they *might* be Eskimo snowshoe prints."

Both boys glanced uneasily about them. The bleak white plains stretched away for miles on every side, and nothing moved on all that white expanse. Just the same Awasin slipped the safety catch off the rifle, and his finger was resting on the trigger.

"It must have been a bear," Jamie said.

"Maybe," Awasin answered. "The Chipeweyans tell stories about the Barrens grizzly and he's a mean animal to meet. I never heard of one being killed, and not more than a couple of Chipeweyans have ever seen one." He shivered, though he was not cold. "Anyway, we don't want to spend the night out here. Let's load up and go home."

In a few minutes they were dragging the sled northward at their best speed.

CHAPTER 19

Gifts from the Dead

THE PRESENCE OF WOLVERINES AT
Stone Igloo Camp was enough to make the boys anxious
to see all their food supplies recached within sight and
sound of the cabin. The inexplicable and frightening
tracks made them doubly anxious to clean out the caches
by the deer fence so that there would be no further need to
visit the place.

In the next three days they made three round trips,
bringing back heavy loads of meat and fish each time. The

167

journeys were uneventful — for which the boys were thankful — but they were ordeals of backbreaking labor. The trips home, dragging the heavily laden sled up the long slopes to Hidden Valley, became a nightmare.

By the time they had started home for the fourth time they were so exhausted that they could only pull the sled a few hundred yards at a time before being forced to stop and rest. Seeking an easier route, they had stayed close to the lake shore this time, intending to circle north, then back to the entrance of the valley, and so avoid the snow-free rock ridges in between. This route took them farther north than they had ever been before and they stared about them, as they rested, with particular interest. It was Awasin's keen eye that first caught sight of a strange object on a ridge ahead.

He pointed toward the crest of a long finger-ridge that ran out at right angles from the hills which cradled Hidden Valley. "What's that queer bulge on the hilltop?" he asked.

Jamie stared in the direction Awasin was pointing. The sun on the snow was blinding, but after a time he made out something that might have been a mound of stones on the very crest of the ridge.

"It looks like any other pile of rocks to me," he said.

"Not any pile," Awasin replied sharply. "Whatever it is, it was made by men."

Despite his fatigue, Jamie grew interested. "We could leave the sled and walk on a way for a better look," he suggested.

Rather warily they went forward. As they approached the ridge, the shape on its summit grew more distinct. Jamie's curiosity mounted and he burst out with, "Looks like the Stone House on the Kazon!" He could have bitten his tongue out the next instant, for Awasin reacted as Jamie might have known he would.

Stopping abruptly, Awasin said, "Let's get out of here!"

If the boys had not been so weary, Jamie might have agreed. But he was tired and irritable. And having come this far, he was determined to climb the ridge and see for himself what the mysterious object was. "Come on!" he said shortly. "A bunch of rocks can't hurt you."

Awasin's mouth set stubbornly. He did not like the implication that he was afraid, but he was not going to give in.

"Go ahead if you want," he said, and there was an overtone of anger in his voice. "I'll wait."

Without a word Jamie turned his back on Awasin and walked on. He did not want to go alone, but he was too stubborn to admit that he also felt uneasy. After going a hundred yards he paused and looked back. Awasin was sitting on a rock, watching him.

"Come back, Jamie!" he called. "It's getting late and we've got a long pull yet to the cabin."

Awasin's words gave Jamie a chance to back down gracefully, but he chose to ignore the opportunity. Stubbornly he resumed the climb.

In fifteen minutes he had gained the ridge and found it swept clear of snow by the north wind. Directly ahead of

169

him was a beehive-shaped mound of rocks, and on the reverse slope of the hill were three more similar mounds.

Feeling even more uneasy, Jamie examined the nearest mound. It was about three feet high and perhaps five feet across the base. Lying near it in the windswept gravel were many fragments of gray and weathered wood. They were hard and brittle as old bones. Jamie picked up a length that was about the thickness of a pencil, and as he pulled it free of the gravel his eye caught a flash of green. He knelt down and a few moments later he was holding an arrowhead in his gloved hand. It was obviously of copper that had turned green with the years. Diamond-shaped, it had been sharpened on all four edges and even now it looked deadly.

Jamie dropped it into his carrying bag and began to scrutinize the ground closely. In a few minutes he had discovered a copper axhead, and a whole series of bone tools and ornaments that were so old they crumbled into dust as he tried to pick them up. There were other implements of copper as well, many of them in odd shapes.

His curiosity had now overcome his uneasiness, even though he suspected that he had stumbled on an ancient graveyard of some forgotten native tribe — perhaps primitive Eskimos of long ago. Jamie knew that it was the custom of the northern natives to place all of a man's possessions on his grave so they could be used by the spirit in the next world. Clearly the tools lying in the gravel had been intended for men whose bones probably lay under the rock mounds.

Jamie glanced down the slope to where Awasin waited and he felt more at ease. Rapidly he circled the grave mounds. Beside one of them he found a squarish block of stone that had been hollowed out and smoothed to a high finish. Further search revealed three more of these stone "pots," and Jamie placed them all in his bag.

A gust of wind struck the exposed crest and drove eddies of snow up the north slope like fantastic shapes of unreal beings. Despite himself Jamie shivered, and turning away from the graves made his way quickly down the hill to where Awasin waited for him.

"Well?" Awasin asked. "What was it?"

Cautiously Jamie replied. "Oh, just an old campsite of Eskimos, I guess. All cluttered up with queer stone tools and copper gadgets. I picked some of them up. We can look them over tonight when we get home."

Awasin was not fooled. He had guessed the real nature of the "campsite" and there was a grim, unfriendly look on his face as he led the way back to the sled. He said not a word all the rest of the weary way home, and the silence between him and Jamie was strained and unhappy.

The cabin was bitter cold when they arrived but soon the fire was roaring and supper was cooking. Jamie bustled about making tea and trying to break through his friend's stubborn silence. He knew perfectly well that Awasin all his life had heard men speak of ghosts and devils as if they really did exist. Superstition or not, Awasin was only obeying the laws of his people when he shrank from any contact with the dead. And Jamie knew that out of sheer stubbornness he had needlessly disturbed his friend.

Trying hard to break through Awasin's mood, Jamie dumped the contents of his carrying bag on the floor and said cheerfully, "Let's have a look at the stuff. Some of it might be useful."

It was the wrong thing to do. The sight of the objects taken from the graves made Awasin's face darken. He lay down on his bunk. "Robbing the dead is evil," he muttered and turned his face to the wall.

Jamie felt as if an unseen barrier had fallen between them. It was a frightening feeling. All of a sudden the immense weight of the loneliness of life in this desolate place seemed to fall upon him. He could not stand it.

He walked to the bunk and put his hand on his friend's shoulder.

"I'm sorry, Awasin," he said. "Maybe you're right the way you think. Maybe there *are* things out there that we don't know much about, and that don't like to be disturbed. I won't do it again."

Awasin rolled over and looked at Jamie. He smiled suddenly. "No!" he said firmly. "*I'm* the one who should be sorry. All this about ghosts! Let's have a look at what you found."

The barrier had vanished. The frightening gap between the two boys, born of their first serious quarrel, was closed. Happily they bent their heads over the assortment of things Jamie had dumped out of his bag.

Awasin picked up one of the stone dishes and examined it closely. He ran a thumbnail down the side of it and

172

found it was soft and soapy to the touch. Absently Awasin handled the dish but he was thinking hard.

At length he spoke. "The other night you wished we had a lamp, Jamie," he said. "Well, I think we've got one!"

Jamie looked surprised. "That old thing?"

"Wait," Awasin replied. He got up and pulled a handful of moss out of a crack in the cabin wall. Expertly he twisted it between his fingers until he had what looked like a three-inch length of rope. Next he took a piece of deer suet, melted it in the frying pan, and poured the grease into the stone vessel. Taking a chip of wood he fastened the "wick" to the chip and put it into the lamp. The wood kept the tip of the wick floating in the hot grease. "Let's have a light," he said to Jamie, who had been watching, fascinated.

Jamie handed him a bit of burning wood from the fire and Awasin touched it to the top of the wick. A fat yellow flame leaped up, smoked hard, and then began to die down.

"I'll have to trim it," Awasin said. He adjusted the wick into a flat, broad strip and relit it. This time the flame burned steadily and hardly smoked at all. The interior of the little cabin was transformed as if by magic. After having been without any real source of light for months, Jamie felt as if someone had switched on a dozen electric light bulbs.

He was delighted. "That *really* makes this place feel like home," he said with enthusiasm.

Awasin grinned with pleasure at his own success. Forgetting his distaste for using things taken from graves, he began to dig through the rest of the relics. His interest focused on one of the copper arrowheads. "This is a queer shape," he said. "It looks as if it was held to the shaft with pegs of bone. There's still a peg left in this one."

"I wonder if *we* could make a bow and arrow that would work," said Jamie.

"We could try," Awasin replied. "I counted the shells yesterday and we only have twenty left. We can't use them on anything except big game. But if we had a bow we could kill ptarmigan and hares."

"The first day we get the chance we'll try and make one," Jamie said. "But not tonight. I'm done for. Let's go to bed."

Sleepily the boys climbed into their robes without bothering to blow out the little lamp. In a few moments they were asleep.

The fire burned down, and from the table shone the gleam of a light that had been reborn after a hundred years of darkness. Once an Eskimo woman must have treasured the little soapstone lamp and over its moss wick cooked food for her family. Now it lived again. And the arrow points that had belonged to some long-forgotten hunter of the dim and dusty past were also ready for new life.

The dead out on that lonely, wind-swept ridge were friendly spirits. They had made gifts to the living of another race, across a century of time.

CHAPTER 20

Winter Strikes

SOMETHING COLD AND WET SWISHing across his face brought Jamie out of the depths of a heavy sleep. He groaned and thrust out his hand. His fingers closed on the stiff, hairy mat of the little fawn's forehead and unwillingly he opened his eyes.

The cabin was as cold as death and almost as dark as night. The lamp had long since burned out, and the fire had sunk away to a few glowing coals. The fawn Otanak was standing by Jamie's bed grunting anxiously, and as

175

Jamie lay still, the fawn thrust its head forward and slapped its tongue over his face a second time.

Jamie sat up abruptly and pushed the little deer away. "Ugh!" he said, wiping his face. "Lay off that stuff!"

He was fully awake now and he began to realize that the usual silence of Hidden Valley had been broken. To his ears there came a steady, roaring sound as if there were a waterfall near the cabin.

Though it was dark, Jamie's stomach — and the fact that the fire had almost burned out — told him it was morning. He jumped out of bed and pulled on his clothes. The cold was terrible and he was blue with it by the time he reached the fire and had begun heaping fresh kindling on the coals. The fawn followed him, nuzzling his back until Jamie in some irritation gave it a shove. "What's eating you, anyway?" he asked.

The fire flared up and Jamie walked to the door to have a look outside and find what was responsible for the rising blare of sound that seemed to be pouring into the cabin from all directions.

He opened the door and a gust of wind almost tore it out of his hands. Snow drove into his face so hard it almost blinded him. He could see nothing except a gray, swirling haze of driven snow, and even the nearby spruce trees were completely obscured. Jamie stumbled back into the cabin gasping for breath.

He shook Awasin awake. "Get up!" he cried. "The granddaddy of all blizzards is blowing. I never saw anything so bad!"

Jamie's description of the blizzard did not do it justice. Roaring down over the darkened plains from the arctic seas, the first real gale of winter had come upon the land. Screaming in wild rage, it hurled itself with the force of a hurricane across the Barrenlands. It scoured the hard-packed drifts, lifting the frozen particles of ice and whirling them into frenzied motion. The snow drove with the force of a sandblast and nothing could face its fury. Wolves and foxes had long ago sought shelter and crouched shivering in holes dug deep under the drifts. Even the ptarmigan were huddled forlornly in rock crevices in order to escape the fury of the gale. No living thing dared stir upon the tortured face of the plains that day.

In Hidden Valley the full force of the blizzard was held back by the protecting mountains, but even in this sheltered place the storm was more than a man could face. The shrieking of the wind across the crests of the surrounding hills was like the constant screaming of unleashed demons. The boys soon found that their cabin refused to warm up until they had blocked the air vent in the floor and spent an hour repacking all the cracks between the logs with moss taken from their mattresses.

Fortunately they had a good supply of firewood laid in with which to fight the cold that they figured had dropped to thirty or forty degrees below zero. They had the fat lamp too, with which to drive away the darkness that the storm brought with it.

After much hurried activity they finally had the cabin snug and almost warm again, and could relax and listen to

177

the fury of the gale outside as it beat its way through the moaning branches of the spruces.

"Imagine what it would have been like if we'd stayed at Stone Igloo Camp," Jamie said, shivering at the thought.

"I'd rather not," replied his friend. "It's bad enough here. But we can take it, as long as our food and wood hold out. And one thing, no wolverines are going to bother our caches in this weather!"

Throughout that day and the next night, the blizzard raged unabated. By the second morning the boys were feeling its effects. Restlessness was upon them, and the constant whine of the gale had begun to irritate their nerves. Jamie felt as if he were trapped under an avalanche, and he could not sit still in one place for more than a few moments.

"I wish we had more things to do," he burst out suddenly. "This sitting around drives me crazy. If we only had some books or games, it wouldn't be so bad."

Awasin had busied himself making some new moccasins and he glanced up at his friend. "Why not have a try at the bow and arrows?" he suggested.

Jamie brightened. It was something to occupy his mind, and moreover it was a challenge to his ingenuity. There were half a dozen spruce saplings that had been cut for the sled and not used which were piled beside the door. Jamie carried them to the fire and looked them over. Finally he chose one about six feet long and two inches thick that appeared to be free of serious knots.

"Do you know how to make a bow?" Awasin asked.

"I've never made one, but I've used them at school for archery practice," Jamie replied. "Don't you know how?"

Rather shamefacedly Awasin replied that he didn't. "You see," he explained, "my people haven't used bows for fifty years — not since they got guns. Sometimes we boys used to make them just for fun but they never worked. It's funny you should know how when we've forgotten."

"I didn't *say* I knew how," said Jamie cautiously. "But I can try at least."

Before he could begin work there was an interruption. Jamie felt a cold blast of air strike the back of his neck, and he turned around to see Otanak happily munching a wad of moss that he had pulled from the wall. The gale whirled in through the crevice and at once the cabin became colder.

Jamie jumped to his feet, shouting angrily, and ran to plug the hole. Otanak skipped nimbly out of the way, and a burst of laughter from Awasin made Jamie turn in time to see the fawn cheerfully yank a patch of moss from the opposite wall.

Even Jamie could not resist grinning. The fawn had resolutely refused to go outside into the storm, and not unnaturally it was getting hungry. It glanced slyly at the boys out of the corners of its eyes, perfectly aware that it was up to devilment — but daring them to try and stop it.

"I guess we have to feed the beast or freeze to death," Awasin said. "Somebody's mattress is going to disappear."

179

"Toss you for it," Jamie replied, and taking one of the copper arrowheads, he made a scratch on one side and flipped it into the air.

Jamie won, and a few minutes later Awasin looked sadly on as the fawn began a big breakfast on the soft moss which had once been Awasin's mattress.

With Otanak occupied, Jamie went back to his bow making.

Using the hatchet, he rough-shaped the stave to about an inch and a half in diameter at the center and half an inch at the ends. He flattened the outside surface, but left the inside curved so that the bow — in cross section — was half-round. With the rough work done, he took a knife and finished off the shaping, being very careful to keep both ends of the bow the same thickness and length so that it would be balanced. Finally he took a piece of sandstone and smoothed off all the rough places.

This job took him most of the day, and he was so engrossed in it that he quite forgot to notice the steady beat of the blizzard.

After dinner Jamie notched the ends of the bow, and placing one end on the floor, he put his weight against the other to test its spring. It bent far more easily than he had expected and he lost his balance. There was a sharp crack, and Jamie sat on the floor with the bow — broken neatly in half — lying beside him. The accident made him feel so disgusted that he almost cried.

"Green spruce isn't very good wood for a bow," Awasin said in an effort to cheer Jamie up a little. "I think my people used to use birch or some other wood they got from the south. But perhaps we could use spruce if we strengthened it some way."

"The heck with it!" Jamie replied. But before he went to bed his stubborn streak and his pride had made him reconsider Awasin's idea. Already Jamie was planning another try.

By the third morning the blizzard had fallen off a little, though it was still too strong to allow the boys to venture out. Jamie began work on a new bowstave while Awasin watched him thoughtfully. In Awasin's hand was a piece of the tough sinew with which he had been sewing moccasins. He stretched it idly; then an idea began to take form in his head.

"Jamie," he said suddenly, "I've got an idea. I remember hearing that the Chipeweyans made spruce bows — it was the only kind of wood they had — and strengthened them somehow with sinew. It's strong stuff and elastic. Want to try it?"

"Sure," Jamie replied. "Why not?"

Now both boys went to work. After much discussion they decided to fix several inch-wide bands of sinew along the outside curve of the bow, then lash the strips firmly to the wood for the bow's full length. They wet the sinew first, and after it was in place on the new bowstave they dried it carefully before the fire.

The results were excellent. The bow was much more resistant, and it took a good strong push on one end to bend it.

"It may work yet," Jamie said hopefully as he tested it. "But what do we do for a bowstring?"

"That's easy," Awasin replied. "I'll braid you one."

Taking a dozen long sinew threads he went to work, and before suppertime he presented Jamie with a braided sinew string so strong that neither boy could break it. Jamie tied a loop at each end of the string, bent the bow, and strung it.

"Try," he said proudly to Awasin.

The Indian boy took it carefully, and drew the string back with all his power. Then he let it go and it twanged against the wood with a really satisfactory snap. He grinned. "The ptarmigan had better watch out," he said. "*After* we learn to shoot. And *after* we make some arrows."

For a moment Jamie looked downcast. "I forgot about the arrows," he said. "We'll have to wait for the next trip to Stone Igloo. There are some willows in the igloo there that should be fine for arrow shafts. Meanwhile I guess we stick to the rifle."

Pleased with themselves all the same for having at least made the bow, the boys turned in. When they woke the next morning, Otanak was anxious to get outside and so they knew that their first winter blizzard had come to an end. The silence that followed the death of the long wind was so complete it made the boys feel like whispering.

Freed from the captivity in the cabin, they could hardly wait to put on their heavy fur clothing and make a journey. With breakfast finished they hurriedly gathered their gear together and prepared for another sled trip to Stone Igloo Camp.

182

CHAPTER 21

A Welcome Discovery

THE LIGHT OF THE LATE DAWN WAS creeping up the arctic sky as they set off. They had gone only a few yards when Jamie noticed that the fawn Otanak was not with them.

Jamie began calling the young deer, but his voice echoed eerily from the silent hills and there was no sound of small hoofs beating on the hard snow.

Awasin looked worried. "I don't like it," he said. "After that storm the wolves will be starving, and he'd be easy pickings for them."

"Let's track him," Jamie said. Leaving the sled where it was, they picked up the rifle and began looking for the prints of little hoofs. These were not hard to find. Even on the solidly drifted snow of the valley, the fawn's sharp hoofs had left clear marks.

The boys followed the trail to the westward, in the direction of Caribou Pasture, as they had come to call it. They had gone about a mile when several new sets of tracks appeared alongside those of the fawn. At the sight of these, Jamie felt his heart begin to beat painfully. The scratches in the snow were the marks made by the claws of wolves.

Without a word both boys began to run. They reached the esker and ran, gasping, up its steep slope, still following the trail.

The light was dim, but as they gained the crest they saw a sight they would never in their lives forget. Far up the valley a circle of dark forms moved on the snowy slope of a tiny hillock. As they stared, there came to their ears the long, lonely cry of a wolf, and it was instantly followed by a chorus of growls and short howls as the shadows seemed to flow and twist like currents in a dark and sullen river.

Jamie felt a sob catch in his throat. He did not need to hear Awasin's words to know that it was over.

"He's gone," Awasin said, and the next instant the roar of the rifle reverberated from the hills about.

Like shadows still, the shapes upon the distant hillock seemed to fade into nothingness and vanish. The range was too far for a good shot, and Awasin did not feel justified in wasting any more of the precious ammunition. With Jamie at his side, he ran forward to the place where the wolves had made their kill. For a long moment they looked down at Otanak, then with unabashed tears in

184

their eyes they turned away and walked slowly back to the sled.

Rage and sorrow were mixed in Jamie's heart. Otanak had meant much to them, for he had helped immeasurably to dispel the great emptiness of the world they lived in. Jamie was not prepared for what Awasin had to say.

"Best forget about Otanak, Jamie," Awasin said. "No use blaming the wolves. If anybody is to blame, it's us. It almost always happens when you take a wild animal and make a pet of it. Sometime or other it has to face up to what its wild brothers meet every day — and then it doesn't know enough to help itself. Sooner or later something like this was sure to happen."

Jamie replied with bitterness, "All the same, I'd like to get a sight on those wolves. I'd make them pay for it!"

Awasin did not answer until they had picked up the pulling straps and were again moving slowly down the valley. Then he said, "Wolves have to eat. What difference is there between their killing the fawn and our killing a dozen does?"

Jamie had no answer for that, and as he thought about it he could see the justice in what Awasin said. His anger against the wolves faded, but he knew it would be many long months before he forgot the little fawn Otanak.

When they emerged on the plains the boys found that the Barrens had again changed its face. The ferocity of the gale had stripped the snow away from all the ridges and hills and piled it in the valleys where it was packed as hard as wood. It was so hard that their feet made no mark on it, and the sled pulled as if it were on greasy ice. The cold was intense, but without wind, and it did not seriously affect the boys. The rising sun made the white world brilliant and almost pleasant.

Still depressed, the boys wasted no time at Stone Igloo Camp, but after laboriously chopping the hard snow away from a cache, they loaded the sled and were soon ready to set out for home. It was lunchtime then, so they pulled out some cold roast meat that they carried in their traveling bags under their parkas — where it would not freeze — and gulped it down. They had begun to move away when a flicker of movement caught Jamie's eye.

"What's that!" he cried sharply — for an instant memory of the mysterious tracks had flashed into his mind.

Awasin too had seen something, and he already had the rifle out of its skin case. The boys dropped to their knees, and knelt, with rapidly beating hearts, staring into the snowy wastes just west of camp. The flicker of movement came again and two shapes appeared silhouetted on a nearby ridge.

"Wolves!" Jamie muttered with a feeling of relief. Then, recalling Otanak, he reached over, grabbed the rifle, and was taking aim when Awasin stopped him.

"Wait!" the Indian boy whispered. "They don't look like wolves."

The two animals were now in full view on the crest. They were certainly wolflike, but they did not seem quite big enough or quite the right shape for wolves.

186

Awasin's keen eyesight made out the difference. With tense excitement in his voice he said, "Those aren't wolves. They're *dogs!*"

Cautiously the boys stood up, while the animals remained motionless a few hundred feet away. Jamie was convinced. "They're dogs all right," he answered, "but what a size! Half again as big as the Huskies down south." He clutched Awasin's arm. "We've got to catch them," he said urgently. "With those two we can have a team — and a chance to get away from here!"

Awasin nodded his head. "We have got to be careful not to scare them, though," he said. "Most likely they've got lost from some Eskimo camp — they look like Eskimo dogs. If they've been lost long they must be nearly starved. Particularly after that blizzard."

"They must have smelled our meat cache," Jamie replied. "Let's see if they'll take food."

He hurriedly chopped off some pieces of frozen meat from the sled load. Then, very slowly, they walked toward the two motionless animals. The dogs did not stir, and when the boys were fifty feet away they saw the black and white markings, big broad ears, and square ruffs of two magnificent Huskies. Magnificent they were — but very timid too.

Suddenly they both turned and bolted with their tails between their legs. They did not run far. One stumbled and fell down. It lay there, struggling weakly.

Even more carefully the boys walked forward again. The fallen dog made a supreme effort and scrambled to its feet.

187

It seemed too weak to run, but it was prepared to defend itself. It turned up its lips and snarled at the approaching boys.

"Good dog," Jamie said soothingly, "good fellow. Come on, boy, have some grub."

"That's close enough," Awasin said warningly. "If we scare them now we'll never see them again. Drop the meat and come back to the sled."

A few minutes later the boys sat on the sled and watched while the two dogs cautiously approached the meat and finally flung themselves on it with ravenous appetites. Frozen as it was, they gulped it down in seconds. One of them raised its head and took a long steady look at the boys; then both dogs turned and walked away to vanish beyond the drifts.

"They're going away!" Jamie cried.

"Don't worry," Awasin soothed him. "We'll head for home now, and I'm certain those dogs will follow, though we won't see a trace of them. They know they can get food from us now."

It was well after sunset when the boys unpacked the sled beside the little cabin.

While Jamie started dinner, Awasin took a bag of meat scraps and walked down the valley. On the way back he dropped bits of meat every few yards. He saw no sign of the dogs, but he was sure they were somewhere near.

That night as the boys lay in their sleeping robes Awasin sat up, his ears straining. From somewhere near came the indistinct sound of an animal snuffling. He whis-

188

pered, "I told you so, Jamie! In a week's time we'll be driving a dog team!"

During the next two days they caught only fleeting glimpses of the beasts, but each morning the meat left on the doorstep had vanished. On the third morning Jamie opened the cabin door before dawn, and a sudden scurrying told him that the dogs had spent part of the night curled up in the little log porch the boys had built to keep the snow out of the house.

Now Jamie had an idea, and when he had explained it Awasin enthusiastically helped put it into action. They spent an hour making a frame of spruce saplings that would fit the entrance to the porch. They hinged this at the top with strips of rawhide, then swung it outward and supported it on a slim pole set in the snow. A long piece of *babiche* ran from this pole through a slit in the cabin door, and was tied to a peg on the inside wall. The whole affair was really only a large box trap set so that the boys could trip it from the cabin and catch the dogs in the outer porch.

That night they baited their trap with several whitefish, then they sat silently and waited. An hour passed before they heard faint noises in the porch. Jamie tiptoed to the wall peg and untied the strip of *babiche*. Tensely he waited until chewing sounds told him that the dogs were occupied with their supper.

A sudden jerk on the line, and the spruce door fell with a great bang. Instantly pandemonium broke loose in the porch.

189

"Light the lamp!" Jamie yelled.

When the cabin was illuminated once more they looked at one another with broad smiles on their faces. "Well, we got them!" Jamie said happily.

Awasin's smile slowly faded and left him looking a little foolish. "But what do we do now?" he asked.

The look of dismay on Jamie's face as he realized what Awasin meant was so funny Awasin couldn't help chuckling. They had thought only of catching the dogs — not of what would follow. The dogs were in the porch and the boys could not get out except by passing through the porch themselves.

"This is a mess," Jamie said ruefully. "Guess I was too smart. How are we going to get out of here without opening that door?"

"No way," Awasin replied. "All we can do is open the door and hope for the best. But wait — I'll make a couple of rawhide nooses and if we're lucky we can slip them over the dogs' heads. If we're lucky!"

When the nooses were ready, Awasin stationed himself by the fire with a noose in one hand and a chunk of spruce in the other for a club. Jamie raised the wooden latch of the door, swung it open a few inches, and jumped behind it.

The two dogs were throwing themselves about the tiny porch like mad things, and neither boy could guess what the Huskies would do when they saw the door opened.

What happened was — silence. All movement ceased and there was not a sound while long seconds passed and

190

the boys waited nervously. At last Jamie peered around the edge of the doorway.

The dogs were crouched together, huddled into one big ball of fur from which four eyes gleamed fearfully. As Jamie peered at them he heard a whine — a sound about as ferocious as a fox terrier pup might make.

"They don't act dangerous!" Awasin said a little shakily. "Let's leave the door open wide and see if we can make friends with them."

For the next hour they coaxed the dogs with pieces of cooked meat and with gentle words. At last one Husky crawled a few feet forward on its belly. Its ears were flat against its broad head, and it was fawning abjectly.

Jamie threw it a scrap of meat, and after a moment the dog gulped it down. Then its huge and bushy tail wagged almost imperceptibly.

That was the turning point. The rest was only a matter of time. By midnight both dogs had left the porch and crawled timidly into the cabin, where they ate themselves into repletion. Gratefully the boys closed the door — for the cabin had become as cold as an icehouse — and heaped up the fire. When they went to bed the dogs were curled up in a corner, cocking an eye occasionally at the boys in case of danger.

During the whole of the next day neither boy made any effort to touch the dogs. After supper Awasin turned his hand to whittling some arrows from a bunch of straight willow sticks brought up from Stone Igloo Camp. Jamie squatted by the fire sewing himself a new pair of deer-hide mitts. It was warm and comfortable and quiet in the cabin.

Engrossed in his job, Jamie forgot about the dogs. Suddenly he felt a cold nose touching the nape of his neck.

At the same moment Awasin said quietly, "Sit still, Jamie — he's sniffing you!"

It was the longest minute Jamie had ever lived. At every instant he expected to feel those long white fangs. But what he felt instead was a hot, wet lick as the Husky ran its tongue over his ear. Cautiously Jamie turned his head. The big dog was standing behind him, its great tail waving slowly back and forth. It looked at him out of huge yellow eyes, then with a sigh lay down, curled up, and put its nose under its tail. It was content. It had found not only food and a home — but a master as well.

In two days' time the dogs were tame. But they were still nervous of sudden movements, and the boys patted them and handled them with care, avoiding any hurried actions. The bigger animal, which weighed nearly a hundred pounds, was a male, and he attached himself particularly to Jamie. The smaller dog was a female. Awasin soon made friends with her.

Now the loss of little Otanak was made good. The presence of the dogs in the camp dispelled the loneliness of the land as nothing else could have done. The boys had a fresh interest in life, and they devoted themselves to the Huskies, who — if all went well — might be the means of delivering them from the winter Barrens.

192

Jamie decided to call the male Fang, while Awasin called his dog Ayuskeemo, which is the Cree word for Eskimo.

It was clear these *were* Eskimo dogs, for they were much bigger than the Huskies used inside the forests. This fact gave the boys, and Awasin in particular, some uneasy moments, for somewhere not too far away there must be an Eskimo camp. Still, it was possible the dogs had been lost and wandering for many days, and they might easily have traveled a hundred or more miles.

Not even a vague fear of the Eskimos could really dim the pleasure that the boys took in their dogs. Fang and Ayuskeemo brought a new atmosphere into the camp, and a new happiness into the hearts of the two boys.

CHAPTER 22

The Great One of the Barrens

IN A WEEK'S TIME AWASIN'S PROPH-
ecy about owning a dog team had come true. While the
boys had been taming the beasts, Awasin had spent some
spare time making two sets of harness. They were of a
simple type having a belly, breast and back strap, but no
collar.

194

One day the boys got their sled down from the cabin roof, where they had stored it to keep the wolverines from eating the rawhide lashings. When the dogs saw the sled they began to howl excitedly and to rush in circles about the boys.

"They know a sled when they see one, anyway," Jamie said hopefully. "Let's see what they do when they see the harness."

Awasin brought the harnesses out of the cabin and attached them to the drawropes on the sled. At once the dogs scampered to the front of the sled and stood waiting until Awasin hitched them up. He put Ayuskeemo in the lead, then he tied the knots on Fang's harness. He had hardly finished when Ayuskeemo gave a great bound and in an instant the sled was moving. The dogs tore out of the cabin clearing and went dashing down the slope with the sled careening and bouncing wildly behind them.

When Jamie and Awasin recovered from their surprise, they raced in pursuit.

They caught up with the runaways two miles down the valley. Sled and dogs were all in a tangle, the dogs lying happily in their traces, waiting to be released.

Back at camp, Jamie and Awasin viewed the experiment with mixed pleasure. "We have a dog team all right," Jamie said, "but it's going to be a tough job to teach them to mind in English. Let's run them down to Stone Igloo a few times for practice before we start any long treks."

For the next four days the dogs and the boys worked on the long haul between the camps. Awasin tied an anchor line to the sled — one that trailed away behind, and that could be caught if the dogs began to run. On the return trips the sled was so heavily laden that the dogs had no chance of running away. In four days they made seven trips, and on the last one they brought back all the remaining food cached at Stone Igloo Camp.

The dogs worked with great energy and endurance, and they began to learn to answer the forest-country driving cries — "Chaw" and "Hew" for left and right. They also displayed amazing appetites. Working dogs, in winter, must have an enormous amount of meat or fish to keep them fit, and the boys viewed this new drain on their food supplies with some uneasiness.

It was clear that more meat was going to be needed soon. There were the deer at the head of Hidden Valley of course, but the boys hesitated to kill any of them — partly for sentimental reasons, and partly because the herd of bucks was an insurance against hunger later on.

For this reason, and because they were anxious to make a real trip with the dog team, they decided on a hunting expedition farther afield.

Jamie thought that there might be other protected valleys along the line of hills to the north, where other herds of deer might have remained. So they made preparations for a search that was to last three days. On the sled they packed their food, sleeping bags, camp gear, and a big bundle of firewood.

It was a clear winter morning with a little pale sunlight

falling on the snow when they set out. Dressed in their fur clothes, they looked like Eskimos. Jamie carried the rifle, while Awasin had the bow slung over his shoulder, and in a little skin quiver he had five arrows, two tipped with copper points and three simply of fire-hardened wood.

The dogs pulled at full speed, so that the boys had to trot in order to keep up. The air was so cold it hurt when it was sucked too suddenly into the lungs. Crystals of hoarfrost soon began to form about the edges of their parka hoods. Every now and then Jamie had to rub his nose and cheeks with an ungloved hand to prevent them from freezing.

Cold though it was, it became a beautiful day. The ice on the little lakes cracked and boomed in the grip of the frost. There was not a breath of wind, and sound carried for many miles. The boys could clearly hear the hungry cry of a raven, so high in the sky it was invisible.

Reaching the River of the Frozen Lake, the boys turned north, into new country. For about two hours they followed the river ice. The western hills began to draw in toward the river so that the valley became narrower. The snow underfoot was as hard as pavement and there were no tracks of living things to be seen anywhere.

About noon they stopped for lunch, and while Awasin got a tiny fire going Jamie climbed a slope to see what the country ahead looked like.

It was a breathtaking sight, and lonely beyond belief. As far as the eye could see there was a rolling expanse that

197

looked like a frozen ocean. The hard snow glittered blindingly and not a tree or a stone ridge broke through the white blanket. The atmosphere seemed unreal, as if it belonged to another, older world than ours.

The sight impressed Jamie in a peculiar way. When he climbed down to join Awasin at the fire he tried to express what he felt.

"Down south," he said, "it's as if the world has a roof and walls. But out here it's as if somebody has knocked down all the walls and lifted off the roof. I never knew before how big the world could be!"

"Big — and empty," Awasin replied. "We haven't heard or seen a single thing except a raven since we started. Let's get away from the river and have a look under the hills."

They ate a hurried lunch, repacked the sled, and turned westward to where the rocky hills thrust their snow-free slopes up from the plains. For half an hour they traveled uneventfully, then Ayuskeemo lifted her head and howled. Fang caught her excitement and both dogs threw themselves into the harness and pulled forward as hard as they could.

"They smell something!" Awasin cried warningly. "Maybe deer!"

Running to keep up, the boys kept a keen watch ahead. The hills grew closer and they could see a small blind valley in the face of the gray cliffs. Awasin suddenly spurted ahead, caught the dogs and stopped them.

"Something moving in that gap ahead," he called softly

to Jamie. "Better get the rifle ready. One of us will have to stay here and hold the dogs while the other does the hunting."

Nodding, Jamie levered a shell into the chamber of the rifle, and bending low, began to run ahead. He took shelter behind a low ridge and followed it for a hundred yards before cautiously raising his head above the crest.

He caught a momentary glimpse of a brown shape passing behind some immense boulders. Ducking down again, Jamie ran on to a gap in the ridge. He slid through it and turned south. He did not know what it was he had seen. Already he had learned how easily the eye is deceived by distances in the winter plains. The shape might have been a hare close up, or a caribou a long way off, but Jamie took no chances and he kept under cover.

Now he was close to the hills and he had entered an area of small, steep ridges between which were confused mazes of shattered boulders. Jamie could not see either the sled or the beast he was hunting. Becoming a little confused, he paused to climb a ridge for a better view, and at that moment he heard a distant cry.

He thought he recognized Awasin's voice and he thought he also heard the howling of the dogs — but it was too faint to be certain.

Turning around, he raced back the way he had come until he reached a tall rock which, with much difficulty, he managed to scale. Clinging to the top, he looked out over the plains to the east.

There was the sled, a tiny toy upon the snow. Some distance from it was the minute figure of Awasin — running. Behind him, and not far behind, loomed a figure that sent a chill of fear through Jamie's heart. It was a bear, though such a bear as few men have ever seen. It bulked as huge as a buffalo and it dwarfed the figure of the Indian boy who fled before it.

Appalled by the sight, Jamie hardly noticed the two dogs, loose from the sled, closing in behind the bear. He half jumped, half slid from the rocky pinnacle, and he was running when he hit the snow. One fact kept hammering through his brain. He had the rifle — while Awasin had only the almost useless bow!

With panting lungs and a bursting heart Jamie ran as he had never run before. Once he fell headlong and almost stunned himself. But he was up in the instant and driving on again. His tired legs worked like rusty pistons and he was so dizzy from the effort that he could hardly see.

It seemed to him that hours passed before he staggered up the last ridge and down the other side. The sled was there, a few hundred yards in front of him. A tremendous outcry from the dogs smote his throbbing ears. Dimly Jamie saw that one of them had been hurt and was crawling weakly away from the giant bear while the other dog tried frantically to hold the monster's attention.

Awasin was circling just out of the bear's reach. Jamie tried to shout, but his lungs hurt as if they were full of shattered glass. He only managed a croak, but it was enough. Awasin turned, saw him, and came dashing toward him.

The Indian boy caught Jamie as he reeled and fell. "The gun!" Jamie muttered as he fainted. "Take the gun!"

Great waves of blackness closed in on Jamie then, but faintly he heard the booming crash of a rifle shot, closely followed by three more; then the darkness was complete and Jamie heard no more.

When he came to himself he was securely wrapped in two sleeping robes, lying beside a blazing fire. It was dark beyond the firelight and the northern lights were flickering overhead. His chest hurt so that he could hardly breathe. Jamie tried to roll over. Something stirred and a great red tongue flapped over his face. It was Fang, curled up on the robes beside him.

Awasin, squatting beside the fire, saw the motion and looked up. Relief flooded his face. He grinned broadly and said, "About time you took an interest! Soup's cooking. But first have a look at your new mattress."

Painfully Jamie turned his head. Under the sleeping robes was an immense expanse of coarse brown fur, as long as that on his own head. The fur covered an area as big as a tent and Jamie touched it with amazement.

At that moment Awasin came over to him with the tea-pail full of thick meat soup. "Drink this and you'll feel better," Awasin said cheerfully. "It's a wonder you didn't kill yourself. Running like that in this temperature, you can freeze your lungs! How does your chest feel now?"

Awasin spoke lightly, but he was worried. He knew that men have died from gulping down the frigid arctic air.

Jamie tried to smile. "Hurts!" he said; then, "What happened?"

Relieved to hear Jamie speak, Awasin gladly launched into the story of the fight with the bear.

"Well," he began, "when you were out of sight I took the dogs forward so I could see what was happening. I was ahead of the sled when the dogs began to growl. I thought they were just excited. Finally Fang howled. I turned to quiet him so that he wouldn't scare the game you were after. There, not more than a quarter of a mile away, was the bear. He was coming upwind at a gallop. He must have smelled the meat on our sled.

"I was too scared even to move. The bear reared up on his hind legs. The dogs were going crazy. I yelled for you as loud as I could. Then the bear snorted, dropped down on all fours, and came on at the run.

"Harnessed the way they were the dogs could never have got away, so I cut them loose. Then I ran too. I hoped the bear would stop at the sled and help himself to our meat.

"Well, he didn't! He was right behind me and gaining. I heard the dogs set up an awful racket.

"Then I got winded, and I looked behind. The bear was on his hind feet with the two dogs tearing into him. They're big dogs — but alongside that bear they looked like mice worrying a fox!"

Forgetting his sore chest in the excitement of the story, Jamie sat upright in the robes. "Then what?" he asked breathlessly.

202

"The dogs had the bear stopped," Awasin continued, "but I knew they couldn't hold him long before they would both be killed. I ran back, but the bear never looked at me — thought I was harmless. When I got close, I opened fire with the bow. The first arrow must have gone in a foot, but that bear never even shook himself.

"Then he caught Ayuskeemo the tag end of a blow with his paw and she shot through the air like a snowball and turned over three times when she hit. Fang went crazy when that happened. He got hold of the bear's rear end and just hung on. I had no more arrows, and I was desperate when I heard you coming.

"The rest was easy. I grabbed the rifle from you and began shooting.

"He was tough, but not even he could take that much lead. He dropped down, made a charge at me, then stopped, looked sort of puzzled, and just collapsed.

"That's about all. If Ayuskeemo hadn't been hurt and you sick, I'd have passed right out. But I had to look after the dog and you, so when I stopped shaking I got the fire going. Then I had to skin the bear. If we'd left him till he froze we'd never have got the hide off. I only skinned one side, because I couldn't turn him over."

In the morning Jamie's lungs felt as if they had been seared with a hot iron, but he could breathe more easily and he felt strong enough to head for home. Awasin piled snow blocks over the dead bear, then loaded Ayuskeemo on the sled (for she could not walk) and let Fang pull her.

Slowly, so that Jamie would not need to strain his lungs, they made for home.

By nightfall they were at the cabin, where Awasin put Jamie to bed again, then bound up Ayuskeemo's wounds. Apart from a badly bruised back and two deep gashes on her hip, she was not seriously hurt.

In a week Jamie was able to breathe normally again and could get around without discomfort. Ayuskeemo was soon better too, though she walked stiffly for some time.

When Jamie was again fit to travel, he and Awasin hitched Fang to the sled, and taking towropes themselves, helped the big dog haul in a load of bear meat.

Jamie was truly startled at the size of the carcass. It was bigger than a farm bull, as massive as a buffalo. There could be no doubt that this giant animal was a Barrenland grizzly — a bear that few white men have ever even heard of, let alone seen. Living in lonely isolation on the broad plains, the Barrenland grizzly is king of his world and has no challengers. The few Eskimos in the land avoid the bears and with reason. Weighing half a ton, they are armed with claws two inches long and razor-sharp. Normally they give men a wide berth, and are not ill-natured. It was probably only outright starvation that had forced this bear to tackle the boys, for at this season of the year it should have been in hibernation.

The boys brought home a paw. It looked as if it measured a good ten inches wide, and a foot long. Jamie looked at it with particular interest, and when he was finished his face was grave.

"No grizzly made those queer tracks we saw at Stone Igloo Camp a month ago," he said at last.

Reluctantly Awasin agreed. The boys went to bed that night with fresh memories of the mysterious tracks filling their imaginations with unpleasant dreams.

CHAPTER 23

Escape

NOVEMBER DREW TO ITS CLOSE AND there came a time when the winter exerted absolute mastery over the Barrens. The gales roared steadily down from the polar seas and laid fierce hands upon the plains. For days at a time it was impossible to go more than a few feet from the cabin door, and the boys' world shrank until it was confined within the four walls of their little cabin.

At first they did not mind. They were snug and comfortable and they knew they had enough food to see them through the bad times. For a while it was fun to sit with the two dogs beside the open fireplace and talk, or work at minor jobs while the brutal wind howled angrily outside.

There was very little daylight now. Dawn broke sometime after ten in the morning, and by about three o'clock night lay over the white, wind-swept world again. The drain on the fat lamps the boys had made from the three soapstone pots grew so heavy that their stocks of fat began to sink alarmingly. They had to ration themselves to one lamp, and for only a few hours each day. So there were increasingly long hours when they could do nothing except sit by the fitful light of the fire and talk, or play at Indian games that Awasin remembered.

Jamie learned cat's cradles — complicated figures woven from a long loop of sinew held on the fingertips. When this grew dull the boys spent hours playing *udzi* — a guessing game — with bits of sticks and pebbles. However, this and the other games they knew or could invent did not hold their interest long.

They talked constantly in an effort to drive away a growing feeling of imprisonment and of depression. Jamie told long stories of his school days in Toronto, while Awasin told old Cree hunting tales and legends.

During the brief hours that the lamp was burning, things were easier. The boys busied themselves sewing new skin clothing; repairing bits of gear; making new dog harness; shaping willow arrows for the bow. Then there was wood to cut, water to get, and food to cook. Jamie particularly took pleasure in inventing new ways of preparing the limited kinds of food they had available. He made stews of fish and meat combined. He made a kind of berry sauce one day from some of the dried crowberries. He invented new ways of roasting deermeat, and he even managed a kind of pancake, using pulverized, dried deermeat for flour, and cooking it in marrowfat.

Oddly enough, neither boy missed the staple foods they had been used to in the south. The lack of salt and sugar had bothered them for the first few weeks, but these were now forgotten. The hunger for flour had lasted longer, but after a month on the plains they no longer felt the need of it, and even the thought of hot bannocks no longer distressed them.

Experience had shown them that a well-balanced diet could be maintained on meat, and meat alone, providing — and this was the important thing — that they had lots of fat with the lean meat.

When once or twice short breaks in the foul weather came, they went outdoors, but they did not dare go far from camp for the skies remained overcast with the ever-present threat of new blizzards.

On these outings, Awasin killed a few ptarmigan with the bow and arrows, while Jamie set a dozen rawhide snares and caught two fine arctic hares. These made a welcome change to their diet, but they were only enough to make the boys wish for more.

As the weather worsened, the dogs were forced to spend more time in the cabin. When Jamie was really depressed he would look at the two big, handsome beasts and feel a thrill of hope — for someday he believed the dogs would help them to escape the bleak winter Barrens.

In the early days of their adventure the boys had seldom

talked about home, for they found this only brought on waves of homesickness that took away all will to work and left them miserable and lazy.

However, as the days passed, they found themselves thinking more and more of home.

Christmas was near. Awasin thought of the cheerful preparations which were even then being made for the annual Christmas journey to the other Indian camps. There would be parties for many miles around through the forest country, and dog teams gaily outfitted with bells and strips of bright ribbon would be passing from cabin to cabin. Awasin knew there would be little rejoicing in the house of Alphonse and Marie Meewasin, for the memory of a son whom they believed to be dead would destroy all merriment.

Jamie often thought of his Uncle Angus, and he believed that Angus Macnair must long since have given his nephew up for lost.

One day Jamie counted the notches on the lead plate, and suddenly he blurted out, "It's just a week till Christmas, Awasin. I guess they all think we're dead."

For the rest of that day the boys were sunk in a pit of depression. They moped listlessly about the cabin while the blizzard howled outside. They were suffering an attack of homesickness much worse than any they had experienced before, and this time they could find no antidote for it.

During the next few days when they talked it was always about their chances of escape. The dogs sensed their unhappiness and whined in sympathy. Life was no longer pleasant in the tiny cabin deep in Hidden Valley.

Then, five days before Christmas, came a real change in the weather. The wind died away to nothing. The sun rose and hung low on the horizon, shining clearly. The temperature went up. A front of warm air had pushed into the arctic from the south, bringing with it a false promise of the spring which was, in reality, still five months away.

The effect on the boys was to make them lose all common sense. They went wild with joy, and as they stood in their tattered shirt sleeves outside the cabin they had but one thought between them. At last they could make their attempt at an escape!

They resolutely refused to admit the dangers that they faced. The urge to make the break was so strong that they put out of mind the hard facts of the case.

The facts were these. First, the freakish good weather could not possibly last more than a few days before winter returned full force. Second, in order to succeed, the boys would have to traverse more than three hundred miles of winter-locked country — most of it open plains — to reach the most northerly camps of the Chipeweyans. It could not take them less than two weeks, and would probably take three, even if they could travel every day. This meant that they would have to carry, on their backs and on the sled, well over two hundred pounds of meat to feed themselves and the dogs. This heavy load would slow them down — which in turn meant they would probably need *more* food before they arrived at safety. And this reckoning was based on the assumption of good weather all the way! But three weeks of good weather was an impossibility. They might be held up by blizzards for a week at a time, in the open plains, without fuel, and with food running low!

Reckoned carefully and coolly, they had only a slim chance of surviving such a dangerous journey. But on this day in December they were not thinking coolly. They were hardly thinking at all. The only thing that mattered was that they were going home.

Despite the reckless mood which was on them, they took what precautions they could. They loaded the sled only with the most nutritious foods: marrowfat, pemmican, and dried meat and fish. They took a tent made from three caribou skins. They resisted the desire to take extra bedding and extra clothes, for they knew that every extra pound would count against them. The ax, all of their heavy equipment, the bear hide, even the bow and arrow were left behind.

When finally the sled stood loaded, and the two dogs whined and twitched in their harness with eagerness to be off, the boys stopped and spent a last few minutes sitting by the dying fire in their cabin. Now that the moment had come to leave, they felt the little building tugging at their hearts. Here they had been safe from every danger. Here they had built new lives for themselves out of their own intelligence and skill. Here too, they had learned to be men.

At last Jamie got to his feet, and after a final look to see that everything was neat, and everything protected from the inevitable wolverines, he turned towards the door.

"Let's get going," he said quietly. "It's not forever. Some-day we'll come back again."

Awasin joined him outside and they closed the door and barricaded it.

The sled moved off down the valley with the boys trot-ting behind it, bent low under their heavy packs. At the esker they turned for a last glimpse of the cabin, and the thread of blue smoke from the dying fire hung silently in the still air.

CHAPTER 24

The White Fire

A YUSKEEMO AND FANG PULLED
steadily at the overladen sled, but the runners would not
slide easily, for the snow had softened in the warm
weather. They made such slow progress that they decided
to spend the first night at Stone Igloo Camp.

As they sat under the igloo's frost-encrusted walls they
were still filled with the fever of excitement that had led
them to begin their journey south. Doubts about the wis-
dom of their plan had not been allowed to come to the surface. In imagination the boys could already see and hear
the tumult of celebrations which their arrival at the Cree
camp would touch off.

They slept fitfully, and when morning came the weather
was still clear and warm. The frost of the night had hardened the snow, so that they made good progress in the
early part of the day.

Because of the dangers of getting lost in this vast wilderness, where all the landmarks were now covered under snow, they had decided to retrace their original route eastward almost to the Kazon. Then they intended to turn south, keeping the river on their left as a kind of fence which would prevent them from straying too far east. Once they reached Idthen-tua Lake they would be able to follow its shoreline, and then turn down the now frozen water route they had followed north early that summer.

During all of the second day they traveled fast and well. By midafternoon they had come up to the great bulk of Idthen-seth Mountain and had swung southward.

It was a queer, hazy sort of day and the snow seemed particularly bright. Jamie complained a few times that his eyes were dazzled by the brilliance, but neither boy paid much attention to the feeling of eyestrain which they experienced.

They steered partly by the sun and partly by the line of the hard snowdrifts, for they knew that the prevailing winter winds were from the north, and so the drifts must run roughly east and west.

No other living things moved on the broad immensity of the frozen plains. Not even the white shadow of a fox, or of an arctic hare, shared the tremendous emptiness with the boys and their two dogs. The boys had, of course, walked the whole distance; and often they had helped the dogs when the eager beasts began to feel the strain. In camp that night the boys looked back on the day's march with pride and confidence.

"Ten more days like this and we'll be at Denikazi's camps," Jamie said optimistically.

Awasin was not quite so confident. Despite their good progress, he knew better than to trust the north too far.

"We'll make it home all right," he replied, "if the weather doesn't break. But we had better count on having to hole up for a few days before we get into timber country."

He paused to rub his eyes and Jamie noticed the gesture. "Do your eyes feel queer too?" Jamie asked. "Mine have been hurting like blazes for the last hour. I wasn't going to mention it, though, until I saw you rubbing yours."

Awasin blinked his eyelids. "Mine feel as if they were full of hot sand," he complained. "We must have strained them today."

It was dark in the little deerskin tent the boys had erected on three spruce saplings which they had carried with them. Awasin got the soapstone lamp, filled it with fat, and lit the wick from a coal raked out of the dying fire. The flame flared up, and instantly a spasm of agony shot through his eyes. He sank back on his sleeping bag almost sobbing with the pain. His hands were sweating and he could hardly speak.

Jamie was farther from the little light. He knelt forward to help Awasin, and the glare of the flame caught him like two swords thrust through his eyeballs.

"My eyes!" he almost screamed. "They're burning!"

On Awasin's face was a look of agony. Tears were running past his swollen eyeballs and coursing down his cheeks. Through waves of pain he managed to speak.

215

"Snow-blind!" he muttered. "We're going blind, Jamie! I should have known. We were fools to walk all day like that without goggles of some kind!"

Jamie did not answer. He had been rubbing handfuls of snow into his eyes in a frantic effort to relieve the pain. It had not helped, and finally he buried his face under his robes to escape even the faint rays of the little lamp.

Awasin was shaken by the knowledge of what the calamity meant. He had heard about snow blindness often, and had even seen one or two men afflicted with it. The White Fire, as the Crees called it, was rare in the forests, where the trees provided shadow and softened the glare of sun on snow. But in the plains it was almost certain to strike any man who had no protection from the sun's rays reflecting from the shining snow, particularly on hazy days.

Awasin knew that there was no cure — except time. For days he and Jamie would have to stay in complete darkness, unable to help themselves. They had been trapped by the very sun they had thought was their friend.

The little fat lamp still flickered, but its rays were no longer seen. As far as the two boys were concerned, the world had become a well of darkness, filled with pain.

The three days which followed were a nightmare. Time passed with terrible slowness. Fang and Ayuskeemo came into the tent, worried and disturbed by the odd behavior of their masters. They whined, and licked the boys, but got no response. At last, driven to desperation by hunger, the dogs tore the covering from the sled and helped themselves to the meat. They gorged, and what they did not eat they scattered about in the deep snow.

Shivering in their robes, the boys were not aware of hunger. Nothing mattered except easing the pain. Gradually it began to lessen, and on the morning of the third day Jamie fell into an uneasy sleep.

When he awakened it was to find Awasin stirring about the tent. "Jamie," Awasin said, "I can see again. How about you?"

Weak from hunger and suffering, Jamie replied, "I can see a little. The pain seems to have gone."

Awasin crawled out of the tent. It was still quite dark, for the sun had not yet risen. Shielding his eyes from the cold air with one hand, Awasin felt his way to the sled to get some meat. He reached it, and for a moment did not believe what his dim eyesight told him. The sled was a shambles, and the supplies of precious food had all but vanished!

It was the final blow. Numbly Awasin stood by the sled and he did not even notice when the two dogs, overjoyed to see him moving about again, came bounding up and thrust against him with their shoulders.

At last he recovered himself a little. He gathered a few handfuls of scraps and took them back into the tent. With the fire drill he laboriously coaxed some moss into flaming life. The light of the flame made him wince, but by narrowing his lids he found he could bear it.

When the scraps of meat were half warmed through Awasin shared them with Jamie, and the two boys ate ravenously.

Glorying in the relief from the pain, Jamie was talkative and even cheerful. He did not notice Awasin's silence and preoccupation.

"That was the worst thing that ever happened to me," he said. "Most of the time I wished I was dead. But we're okay now, and it won't happen twice. Anyway, nothing else that *could* happen to us would be half as bad."

Awasin could keep silent no longer. "There is something worse," he said reluctantly. "The food's all gone, Jamie. The dogs got starved while we were sick . . ."

It was shocking news, and for several minutes Jamie could find nothing to say. Then an idea began to emerge from the confusion of his thoughts. It seemed so clear, so obvious, that he could not understand how it had escaped him for so long. It was perhaps the most important single piece of knowledge that had ever come to him — and it took a near tragedy to drive it home. He had to think about it for a while, but first he did his best to comfort Awasin.

"Well," he said as cheerfully as he could, "that's not so bad. We'll just have to go back to Hidden Valley. We're only thirty or forty miles from it and we should make it in two days."

Awasin brightened. "Yes," he said, "that's the only thing to do. I knew we'd have to go back but I thought that you'd refuse — I'm glad you see the way it is."

218

By now the idea in Jamie's mind had crystallized. He was ready to share it with his friend.

"Yes, we'll go back, Awasin," he said, "and we'll stay at Hidden Valley. Stay there as long as we have to. I've learned my lesson. As long as we went along with things the way they were, and never tried to fight against this country, we were all right. But when we set out on this trip south we were standing up to the Barrens and sort of daring them. We were going to bulldoze our way through. And we're lucky to be still alive!"

Awasin looked long into his friend's face.

"I never thought you'd understand about that, Jamie," he said at last. "White men don't as a rule. Most of them think they can beat the northland in any fight. A lot of them have found out differently, and didn't live to tell about it. My people *know* differently. It's hard to put into words, but I think you understand. If you fight against the spirits of the north you will always lose. Obey their laws and they'll look after you."

It was a long speech for Awasin, but when he finished both boys felt happier than they had for many weeks. They were humbler too. They were ready to return to the tiny cabin in the valley and to abandon their foolish and almost fatal effort to force their will upon the Barrenlands.

They spent the rest of the day at their lonely camp in the empty plains. Carefully Jamie gathered up all the meat he could find about the sled, and it was enough for two days of half-rations. Meanwhile Awasin had taken two broad strips of rawhide, each about two feet long. In these he had

219

carefully cut narrow eye-slits. Bound around the boys' foreheads, these would serve as makeshift snow goggles.

When a half-moon rose that night the boys harnessed up. Soon they were moving north again — back home.

The night was still and cloudless and the cold was sharp. The moon hung low in the sky and the world was a blue immensity of space. They walked slowly behind the sled and occasionally one would ride for a while, for they were still weak from the three days of snow-blind sickness.

Towards midnight the northern lights broke into a riot of color. Curtains of green, yellow and pale red flamed across the sky, and it seemed to Jamie that he could hear a faint rustling sound, like the swish of silken dresses.

Awasin heard the sound too and for a moment he was puzzled, then the answer flashed across his mind. His lips set grimly. He turned to Jamie.

"Perhaps *we've* called it quits," he said, "but the fight isn't over yet. That's wind we hear!"

The memories of the gales that had roared over Hidden Valley in weeks past filled Jamie's mind. "We can't get caught out here," he said urgently. "We've no fuel left and almost no grub."

"Perhaps we can make the shelter of the mountain," Awasin replied.

The dogs too had heard the warning of the approaching storm and they needed no urging. The boys ran and the sled careened wildly over the hummocks and little ridges.

After half an hour of this they had to stop and rest. The dogs whined anxiously and impatiently, and the faint, far-off rustling sound grew in volume until it began to sound like a distant waterfall. Gray clouds obscured the moon and the northern lights faded and died away. The darkness grew thicker so that it was hard to see what lay ahead.

When the sled moved on there was already a light breeze blowing and the temperature had begun to fall abruptly. Awasin automatically noted the direction of the breeze for he knew in a short time it would be his only guide, and he would have to steer by the feel of it alone.

Resting every fifteen or twenty minutes, the boys fled northward. The roar of rising wind now filled their ears and it was mingled with the throbbing of their hearts. The gale gained power slowly until they had to pull their parka hoods forward against its bitter touch. The snow in the hollows began to rise above the hard drifts and whirl like ghostly dancers. Frost thickened on the fur trimming of the parka hoods.

It had become almost pitch-dark. Awasin went ahead to lead the dogs, and when he was a few feet from Jamie he was completely out of sight. Jamie followed close behind the sled, but several times he almost lost it and at last he tied himself to it with a length of rawhide line. Stumbling with fatigue, he managed to keep on his feet only by the greatest effort.

The roar of the gale was now no longer distant. No longer simply warning them, it burst down out of the darkness with full fury. It rose to a soul-shaking crescendo of sound.

The blizzard was upon them!

CHAPTER 25
Peetyuk

Tʜᴇ ᴡᴏʀʟᴅ ʜᴀᴅ ʙᴇᴄᴏᴍᴇ ᴀ ᴡʜɪʀʟ-ing, screaming nightmare of wind and snow. Gasping for breath, Awasin halted and turned his back to the gale while the dogs huddled close to his knees. A moment later Jamie came stumbling up, feeling his way along the sled.

"Got to camp!" Jamie shouted in his friend's ear.

"Can't!" Awasin yelled back. "Freeze to death out here. Go that way!" He pointed to the east. "Wind partly behind us then!"

222

Now both boys clutched Ayuskeemo's harness as they stumbled off toward the northeast. Somewhere ahead they hoped to find the protecting shoulders of Idthen-seth, and under its stony flanks there might be shelter. It was the only hope. There was no choice but to go on, for to have camped in the open would have certainly meant death.

The snow whipped down like driven shot and the gale deafened them. For what seemed like endless hours they dragged themselves forward, falling, pulling themselves up again, and staggering on.

At last Jamie fell for the last time. He could not get to his knees and, past caring, he lay back in the snow and gave up trying.

Awasin shook him frantically. "Get up!" he screamed. "You'll die if you lie there! Get up!"

Jamie did not answer. A warm, drowsy feeling was driving out the chill of the blizzard. He drifted off into a dreamy world and imagined that he was at home, far to the south, and someone was tucking him into a warm bed. Who was it? He did not know, or care. The bed was soft and comfortable and he only wished to sleep . . .

For a moment Awasin was panic-stricken, but he kept his head. Summoning his remaining strength, he managed to roll Jamie on the sled and wrap him in the sleeping robes. Then he fought his way back to Ayuskeemo's side and once again took up the terrible struggle with the storm.

Mechanically his legs shuffled on. He hardly noticed when the dogs swerved from their course and began to trot. Awasin was pulled along unprotesting until the dogs stopped short and Fang lifted his head and howled.

Fang's great voice could hardly be heard above the raging wind, but it served to rouse Awasin from his stupor. There was a momentary slackening in the blizzard, and as Awasin raised his head he saw before him, hardly a sled length away, the dim bulk of something round and smooth. A thought slowly came to life in his tired brain. "Igloo!" he thought. "Eskimos!" But he was too far gone to be afraid. Devils or men might own this igloo — but at least it was shelter from the storm. He stumbled forward.

The entrance tunnel was directly in front of him, and falling to his knees, he crawled in. The relief of escaping from the blizzard was so great he almost fainted. Then he remembered Jamie.

Using all the remaining strength in his tough body, he crawled back to the sled, pulled Jamie's limp form to the snow, and tugged him to the tunnel mouth. Inch by inch Awasin struggled forward through the five-foot tunnel until he knew he had reached the igloo's little inner room.

His work was not yet finished. Leaving Jamie, he retraced his steps to the sled, cut the dogs loose from their harness, and gathered up the deerskin robes and the rifle. The journey back into the igloo was the longest of his life, and when he reached Jamie's side it was all he could do to spread the robes and crawl inside them alongside his friend before darkness overwhelmed him too.

The two dogs had followed him in and now they curled

up on the edge of the robes, adding their body heat to that of the two boys, so that in a little while the deadly chill vanished from the air and the wanderers, boys and dogs, slept the sleep of complete exhaustion.

Awasin never knew how long he slept. He woke dazedly and slowly opened his eyes. Above him was the pearl-gray outline of the snow dome, but for some minutes his mind was too drugged to realize where he was. Slowly he recalled the events of the blizzard and the finding of the empty snowhouse. Once again the thought of Eskimos raced through his brain — this time with the effect of an electric shock.

He sat up and stared around him in sudden fright. The igloo was deserted. There was no sound of the storm, for it had died away hours earlier. Thin daylight shone through the snow blocks of the roof and revealed a broad sleeping ledge of snow across one half of the igloo. On the ledge were caribou skins and pieces of deermeat, but there was no sign of a human being.

With one hand Awasin reached for the rifle, while with the other he shook Jamie's shoulder. Jamie moaned a little and slowly came awake. Through his sore and swollen eyes he could see Awasin's face bending over him, and beyond that, the dome of the igloo. "Where are we?" he asked between cracked lips.

Hurriedly Awasin told the story of the last part of the journey, concluding with: "We're in an Eskimo igloo, and

225

we can rest for a while — if the Eskimos don't come home!" He could not repress a shiver at the prospect and again his hand went to the rifle by his side.

The igloo was cold, but not unbearably so, for it had been well made, and freshly cut snow blocks make fine insulation. Stiffly the two boys crawled out of the robes and looked about. Their eyes fell on the meat and hungrily they examined it. It was frozen solid, but in a niche in one side of the igloo was a little stone lamp very much like the ones they had found on the Eskimo graves. It was half full of congealed fat.

Awasin managed to squeeze out through the tunnel to the sled and get the fire drill. The two dogs met him outside and showed by their swollen stomachs that they too had found food.

The sky was clear but hazy, and in the diffused light Awasin could see nothing that looked in the least familiar. The white blanket covering the plains seemed to be unbroken as far as his eyes could reach. Very far off to the northwest was a smoky line that might have been the shape of Idthen-seth, half hidden in snow eddies. But if he could not tell where he was, at least Awasin had the relief of knowing that no other living thing was moving on the plains.

After a hard struggle he managed to get the stone lamp lit, and he and Jamie toasted scraps of deermeat over the little flame until they were partly thawed. They ate and ate, and, as the lamp burned away, the interior of the igloo grew quite warm. At last, gorged and relaxed, they sank

226

back into sleep. With a last impulse of caution Awasin levered a shell into the chamber of the rifle, and placed the gun so that he could grasp it in an instant.

They had not slept many hours when Jamie was awakened by a hoarse growl from Fang, who had curled up by his head. Sleepily Jamie rolled over on his side; then Fang burst into a series of howls that made both boys shoot upright in their sleeping robes.

The dogs stood by the tunnel entrance with their back hairs erect. Suddenly Fang dashed out, close followed by his mate, and pandemonium broke loose outside.

Awasin's face had set in a tight grimace of fear. Squirming out of the robe, he fell on his knees, holding the rifle leveled at the tunnel mouth. Jamie, too, felt his heart pound heavily as he fumbled for the hunting knife slung at his waist.

From outside the igloo a chorus of dog howls had risen to a wild crescendo of sound, punctured by a voice crying strange words. Almost at once the sounds of the dogs ceased and an uneasy silence followed.

"The tunnel! Watch the tunnel!" Awasin whispered hoarsely. Sweat was standing out on his face and his terror was such that the rifle shook in his hands. All the ancient tales of the savagery of Eskimos had awakened in his imagination. Awasin's fear was catching, and despite himself Jamie felt it too.

Now there came a rustling sound from the tunnel and the tension became unbearable. Awasin's finger twitched on the trigger of the rifle.

Jamie felt his heart leap wildly, for a face had suddenly appeared in the dark opening before him.

It was not the face itself that froze Jamie and Awasin into such immobility that neither of them could have moved a muscle. It was the hair that escaped from under the hood of the stranger's parka. Long hair it was — and flaming red in color!

Awasin's voice, high-pitched and unnatural, broke the silence with a yell — and his finger tightened convulsively on the trigger.

Jamie flung himself forward and into Awasin, knocking the Indian boy over on his side. The face in the tunnel mouth vanished, but Jamie was already in hot pursuit. "That was a *boy* you almost shot!" he flung over his shoulder at Awasin as he scrambled out of the tunnel.

As Jamie stood up outside, Fang threw himself against his legs, whimpering with excitement. Jamie shielded his eyes with both hands and there, not fifty feet away, he saw a long sled to which was harnessed a team of a dozen dogs. The stranger stood with one foot on the sled, as if ready to leap aboard and flee. He was dressed all in furs, and Jamie could see that under the mop of red hair there was the frightened face of a boy not much older than himself.

Quickly Jamie thrust out his empty hands to show he had no gun, then he tried a smile. The stranger stood poised like a deer ready for flight.

"Friends!" Jamie cried desperately. "Don't go! We're friends!"

228

It was obvious that the stranger had his doubts — and not much wonder, considering the reception he had met in the igloo. The decision hung in the balance and then Ayuskeemo saved the day.

She had been smelling noses with the big beasts of the stranger's team. One of these dogs became jealous and tackled its neighbor. Next instant the whole team exploded in a roaring free-for-all.

The stranger leaped off the sled and flung himself into the melee. Jamie ran to help, and for a few minutes the two were all mixed up in a mass of snarling, snapping Huskies.

By dint of kicks, wild yells, and adroit bangs on the dogs' snouts, the battle was brought to an end. Then, panting, the stranger and Jamie looked at each other.

The unknown boy was dark-skinned like an Indian, but his features were regular and sharp. His startling red hair was not his only oddity, for Jamie saw that he had clear blue eyes as well. Tentatively now the stranger smiled.

Overjoyed, Jamie pointed to the igloo and made signs of eating. The stranger smiled broadly, and to Jamie's consternation said in English: "Sure — we eat *tutktu* — deer. But that fellow, he act like he want to eat me!" He pointed to the igloo and Jamie, turning, saw Awasin standing openmouthed, staring at him, with the rifle still held in his hands.

Awasin looked remarkably foolish, his mouth open and his eyes fairly popping out of his head.

When Jamie had prevented him from firing the rifle,

Awasin assumed that his friend had gone quite mad. But terrified as he was, Awasin had hurried to save Jamie from the awful fate he was sure awaited him outside. He had crawled out of the tunnel prepared to sell his life dearly in Jamie's defense, and he had arrived in time to witness the dogfight, and to see the dreaded stranger, the Eskimo eater-of-raw-flesh, standing at Jamie's side, grinning merrily, and talking in English!

It was too much for Awasin. The rifle slipped out of his hand and fell muzzle down into the snow while Jamie, unable to contain himself, burst into howls of laughter. The stranger laughed too while Awasin shook his head foolishly as if doubting his own eyes.

An hour later the three boys sat in the igloo eating heartily of the meat which the stranger, who said his name was Peetyuk, produced from his sled.

It took some time for his story to be told, for Peetyuk's command of English was sketchy, and he had trouble making himself clearly understood at first. But by the next day, when the three boys set out from the little igloo in the direction of the Kazon River to find the camps of the Eskimos, Jamie and Awasin had learned much of Peetyuk's fascinating history.

The story began on a day seventeen years earlier, when Peetyuk was born in an igloo of the inland Eskimos not far from the Kazon. His mother was an Eskimo, but his father was a white man — the same white man who had disappeared from Thanout Lake on a trading expedition to the Eskimo country twenty years before. He was the red-

230

headed Englishman for whom the old ruined building at Red-Head Post was named.

The young trader had made his way into the Eskimo country and then had suffered an almost fatal accident when his sled overturned among some ice hummocks. The Eskimos had found him and had taken him to their camps, where he was nursed back to life. In due course he married an Eskimo woman, and a year or two later his son Peetyuk was born.

It had always been the man's intention to take his wife and child back to his own country, but his wounds had never completely healed, and when Peetyuk was only four years old his father died.

Before his death, the sick man did everything he could to make sure that his son would someday return to the land of the white man. He taught Peetyuk's mother to speak English, and he made her promise to teach the boy. She also promised that, when the boy was old enough, he should be sent south to seek his father's people.

Peetyuk's mother had done her best to keep these promises. But neither she nor any of her people had ever dared to journey south into the forests, for they were far more afraid of the Indians than the Chipeweyans were of the Eskimos. So, when he became old enough to travel, Peetyuk had tried to make his own contact with the strange peoples of the south.

It had been Peetyuk, trying to make contact with Deni-kazi's hunting party on the River of the Frozen Lake, who had unwittingly caused Jamie and Awasin to be marooned in the Barrens. But this had not been the Eskimo boy's fault, and whatever trouble he had accidentally caused the two boys he had more than redeemed by saving their lives now.

The reception he had met at the Chipeweyan night camp would have discouraged most people — but not Peetyuk. He still had hopes of obeying his father's wishes. One day when he was on a long trip looking for two lost dogs (the two that Jamie and Awasin found), he came across the Stone Igloo Camp by the shores of the River of the Frozen Lake, and once more his hopes had risen.

Wearing Eskimo snowshoes of deer hide stretched solidly on willow frames, he had tramped about the apparently deserted camp hoping to find some clue that would help guide him back to his father's country. It was the round, unfamiliar track of his snowshoes that the boys had later discovered by their cache.

Peetyuk had not suspected the boys' presence in Hidden Valley, but during the early winter he had roamed the area south of Idthen-seth in the faint hope that he might encounter the people who had made the caches at Stone Igloo Camp. That was the reason that he had built the little travel igloo on the plains, at a central point from which he could roam to the west and south. It was this igloo that had saved the lives of Jamie and Awasin when the blizzard caught them.

CHAPTER 26

The Eaters-of-Raw-Meat

A YEAR EARLIER NEITHER JAMIE
nor Awasin would have believed that one day they would
be sitting in a huge snowhouse surrounded by at least
thirty of the fur-clad people who, for centuries, the Indians had considered to be no better than bloodthirsty sav-
ages. But this is what the boys were doing the day after
their meeting with Peetyuk.

233

Peetyuk had lent them three of his dogs, and with these and with Ayuskeemo and Fang the little sled fairly flew over the hard-packed snows following Peetyuk.

The two sleds headed southeast and they traveled for five hours at an unbroken pace. At length they reached the snow-covered Kazon, which Peetyuk called Innuit-ku —the River of Men. After an hour on the river ice, they rounded a point and came upon a settlement of seven igloos huddled under a high cut-bank.

Nearly fifty dogs broke into a frenzy of excitement as the sleds approached, and from each igloo a crowd of people rushed outside. They came laughing and yelling down to where the sleds had drawn up and they surrounded Peetyuk, while casting curious glances at the two strange boys who stood a little way apart, uncertain what to do.

The Eskimos talked so hard that the babble was deafening, but at last Peetyuk led the way to where Jamie and Awasin waited. Peetyuk beamed at them and waved a hand at the milling crowd that was bubbling over with curiosity and high spirits. "My people. Your friends!" Peetyuk shouted. He beckoned the boys to follow and led the way to the largest of the snowhouses.

The entrance tunnel was ten feet long and only three feet high, so that the boys had to stoop to enter it. Halfway along was a niche built into one wall in which a female husky nursed a litter of newly born pups. On shelves cut in the snow were chunks of meat, and piles of fur clothing.

When the boys reached the igloo proper they stood up

under a dome ten feet high and fifteen feet across. The whole back half of the circular floor was raised three feet high on snow blocks and covered with caribou hides to make a combination couch and bed.

To the boys' surprise, the inside of the igloo was uncomfortably warm, though it was below zero outside. Three fat lamps burned in niches near the wall, and so perfect was the insulation of the snow blocks that almost no heat was lost.

The sleeping bench was soon crowded with people who swung themselves up and sat grinning cheerfully at the newcomers. Foremost of the Eskimos was a sturdy old man with thin, straggling whiskers and a mop of lank black hair. He had a broad, flattened nose and high cheekbones. His eyes were black and almost hidden under his wrinkled forehead.

He stood before the boys smiling at them and he spoke slowly, while Peetyuk translated.

"This place is yours," he said. "Eat with us. Sleep with us. Your home now."

While the old man was speaking, three women appeared from other igloos, each lugging a pot. A big wooden tray was laid on the sleeping bench and into it the women poured boiled caribou tongues, boiled ribs and a thick soup. Another pot nearby held gallons of hot Labrador tea. The Eskimos on the bench made room for Jamie and Awasin, and moved over giggling and laughing as the boys clambered up. "Eat!" Peetyuk said, and set the example by seizing a deer tongue hungrily.

They ate until they could eat no more. Then they leaned back comfortably to listen while Peetyuk told the story of finding the strange boys. Men, women and children crowded into the igloo until it was so full there was hardly room to move. Delightedly they listened, applauding loudly, and nearly laughing themselves into hysterics when they heard how Awasin had greeted Peetyuk.

Now Peetyuk introduced his friends, naming each Eskimo individually. At last he came to the old man who was obviously the owner of this igloo. "Kakut," Peetyuk said. "My father-father."

"He means grandfather, I think," Jamie whispered to Awasin.

Peetyuk reached out and caught the arm of a broad-faced, happy-looking woman. Peetyuk grinned affectionately. "This is my m —" He stopped, forgetting the word. The woman came to his rescue. "Me his mutta," she said smiling. "Fatha dead many winters. White man — like you," and she pointed at Jamie.

When the introductions were finished, Kakut got out a stone pipe and loaded it with some kind of dried leaves. When it was drawing well he passed it to the boys. Neither Jamie nor Awasin had smoked before, but they felt they should make the effort. After a puff or two of the acrid smoke they burst into paroxysms of coughing. The Eskimos watched in amazement for a moment, then began to howl with laughter, rolling on the floor and rubbing their sore stomachs.

"One thing certain," Jamie said a little ruefully to

236

Awasin, "these people act about as dangerous as puppies. They're a darn sight better-natured than the Chipeweyans!"

For many hours the activity in the igloo was sustained. There were songs, there was more laughter than either boy had ever heard at one time before. The boys did their best to be gay too, and Peetyuk worked hard interpreting for them. But at last the heat, the good food and the long journey began to make them so sleepy they could hardly stay awake.

With a few words Kakut cleared the igloo of all except his own family. Jamie was sleepily aware that someone was covering him with a robe, then he drifted off knowing he was among friends.

And so ended the great adventure that had begun at the camps of Denikazi almost six months earlier. In the camps of the inland Eskimos the long months of danger, of difficulty and of loneliness had come to their conclusion.

A week after their arrival at the Eskimo camps Jamie and Awasin were again heading south. But this time they were not alone.

Many conferences with the Eskimos had at last convinced old Kakut that it would be safe for his men to venture into the forbidden lands of the Indians. On a bright January day three sleds raced southward on the frozen Kazon River. First there was Kakut's twenty-foot sled, with Awasin riding on it to act as guide once they left the familiar lands of the Eskimos.

Jamie and Peetyuk followed on the boys' little sled, but with all of Peetyuk's dogs helping Fang and Ayuskeemo. Behind came the sled of one of Peetyuk's older cousins.

The trip was an easy one, for the Eskimos had always known the secret that Jamie learned so belatedly out on the frozen plains when he and Awasin were stricken with snow blindness. The Eskimos knew that they must always travel *with* the forces of the land — and never fight against them.

The party traveled in fair weather only. When storms threatened they halted at once and built comfortable travel igloos in which they could stay for days if necessary. However, the weather remained fairly good, and on the ninth day the black line of the forests appeared on the horizon.

Awasin and Jamie now took the lead and guided the dog teams down White-Partridge River. They swung well around the camps of Denikazi, however, for they suspected that the sudden appearance of the Eskimos would throw the Chipeweyans into blind panic that might result in trouble.

One January afternoon they crossed the broad stretches of Kasmere Lake, and drove up the Kasmere River to the head of Thanout Lake, where they halted for the night.

As the Eskimos built fires of spruce — big, generous fires were a source of surprise and pleasure to them after the "little sticks" of the Barrens — Jamie and Awasin took Peetyuk to the ruins of Red-Head Post. From this place a young man filled with great courage and a desire to ex-

238

plore the north had set out nearly twenty years ago, never to return.

"Your father's igloo," Jamie said.

Peetyuk looked for a long time at the heap of fallen logs, and when he turned away his eyes were glistening. "Peetyuk come home," he said at last, speaking so softly that the boys could hardly hear him.

They did not notice that old Kakut had come up through the darkness. Then the old man spoke, and though Jamie and Awasin did not understand the words they guessed their meaning.

"The son goes to his father's land," Kakut said, "and leaves his mother's land in the place of memories. Peetyuk was my heart's son — but he is of your blood. Take him, and let the love of brothers be between you." Kakut took his grandson's hands and placed one in Jamie's and the other in Awasin's.

Then he smiled gently at the three boys, and turning away, vanished in the darkness.

Jamie awoke the next morning to find Awasin shaking him violently.

"They've gone!" Awasin cried. "Kakut and the other Eskimos have gone!"

It was true. During the night the two Eskimo sleds had vanished silently into the north, leaving behind them Peetyuk and his two new friends. Peetyuk himself was awake and sitting on a nearby log beside a dead fire, staring northward.

Awkwardly Jamie laid an arm over the boy's shoulders.

"Never mind, Peetyuk," he said. "Someday soon we'll all three go back and visit with your mother's people."

Peetyuk stood up and smiled. "That is good," he said. "Now let us go to your people there." He pointed down Thanout Lake, and far in the distance the boys could see the tiny blue smoke plumes of the fires at the cabins of the Crees.

CHAPTER 27

The Return

A YOUNG COUSIN OF AWASIN'S SAW the sled as he was getting water from an ice hole in the lake. He stared hard at the object coming toward the settlement. The wolflike dogs and the strange fur-clad figures looked to him like something from one of the old spirit legends, and suddenly he dropped the pail and fled up the slope.

In a few minutes the shore was lined with people. The men watched the approaching sled uneasily and the children were frankly frightened. The sled was within a hundred yards of shore when Marie Meewasin recognized her son.

What followed was pandemonium. In a moment Marie had caught both Jamie and Awasin against her ample bosom and was almost squeezing the life out of them

241

while she alternated between crying and scolding. Cree youngsters ran screaming the incredible news among the cabins, and the crowd by the sled kept growing until the whole population was gathered there. The cries and questions and shouting made a babble of sound that was nearly deafening.

It was some time before anyone could talk sensibly, but then Awasin caught his father's arm and led him to the sled, where Peetyuk had been sitting timidly during the excitement of the arrival.

"This is Peetyuk," Awasin said. "His father was the trader who disappeared from Thanout Lake. It was Peetyuk and the Kazon Eskimos who saved our lives, and now he has come south to live."

Alphonse's dark face broke into a broad smile. He took Peetyuk's hand.

"Today my son came back from the shadow world," he said. "I know a great happiness because of this. It is the greater happiness because he has brought me yet another son."

The Crees standing near gave a shout of welcome and crowded close to pat Peetyuk on the shoulder. Then with Jamie on one side and Awasin on the other, he was led up to the Meewasin house.

Later that day a toboggan hauled by a dozen exhausted dogs careened into the camp. The driver was an Indian who had been dispatched to Macnair Lake the instant the boys were recognized. With him was Angus. For several

242

minutes the big Scotsman could only clasp Jamie's hand and mutter, "Thank God it's true!"

That night was an endless one. In the Meewasin cabin the stove glowed red while Marie outdid herself cooking piles of golden bannocks and plate after plate of fried deermeat and whitefish. Every chair and bench was occupied and tobacco smoke hung like a fog. The three boys sat near the stove. Surrounding them, the Cree elders and Angus Macnair listened fascinated as the story was told. It was past dawn before anyone had thought for sleep.

The next day, when the excitement had died down a little, Jamie and Awasin learned what had happened after they were lost. They heard how Denikazi had visited Angus and Alphonse and had actually offered his own life in payment for the loss of the boys. Angus told how he and Alphonse had gone north by canoe to Idthen-tua, where freeze-up caught them and forced them to return. Alphonse told of a dog-team expedition under Denikazi's leadership that had continued the search in late November but had found no sign of life. Even as the boys drove into the Cree camp, Alphonse and Angus had been preparing yet another trip, this time to find the fabled inland Eskimos and question them.

The knowledge of the pain their adventure had caused to others cast something of a shadow over the boys' spirits, but it could not last, for everyone was so delighted to see them back that there could be no recriminations.

Peetyuk was not forgotten. Angus had known his father, Frank Anderson, very well and had often stayed with

243

him at Red-Head Post. He was able to tell Peetyuk much about his father and his father's life.

"Frank was a good friend to me," he concluded, "and as for you, Peetyuk, you'll come and live with us as long as you will stay." So it was arranged, and for some years to come Jamie and Peetyuk lived together almost as brothers.

Angus was particularly interested in the boys' story of the Great Stone House, and he examined the lead tablet carefully.

"It will take an expert to be sure," he said when he was through, "but I've no doubt you've guessed correctly about the Vikings. Next summer we'll take a trip to yon Stone House. I've a mind to visit Peetyuk's people too, for I'm thinking I have a debt to pay them. What do ye say, lads?"

What Jamie, Awasin and Peetyuk had to say resulted in many a long winter night spent beside the stove of the Macnair cabin making plans. But as to what came of those plans — that is another tale.